Brittany had already spotted a few male counselors standing around the buses.

"Excuse me." She smiled. "Could any of you help me—"

"Sure can!" came the expected chorus.

An especially good-looking counselor, slightly taller than the others, stepped forward. "The rest of you go about your business. I'll help this little lady."

Brittany dimpled. "Thanks, but this 'little lady' has four not so little suitcases."

He arched a dark eyebrow but didn't falter. Moving back, he rested his arms on the shoulders of the two boys beside him. "I was wrong, guys. This is going to take all of us."

"I'm sorry to be so much trouble." Brittany's eyes passed lightly over the three boys as she included them all in her laughing apology. "I'm Brittany Allen, and, in case you haven't guessed, this is the first time I've ever been to camp."

Dear Readers:

Thank you for your unflagging interest in First Love From Silhouette. Your many helpful letters have shown us that you have appreciated growing and stretching with us, and that you demand more from your reading than happy endings and conventional love stories. In the months to come we will make sure that our stories go on providing the variety you have come to expect from us. We think you will enjoy our unusual plot twists and unpredictable characters who will surprise and delight you without straying too far from the concerns that are very much part of all our daily lives.

We hope you will continue to share with us your ideas about how to keep our books your very First Loves. We depend on you to keep us on our toes!

Nancy Jackson
Senior Editor
FIRST LOVE FROM SILHOUETTE

SPOILED ROTTEN
Brenda Cole

First Love from Silhouette

Published by Silhouette Books New York

America's Publisher of Contemporary Romance

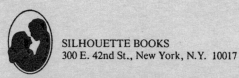

SILHOUETTE BOOKS
300 E. 42nd St., New York, N.Y. 10017

Copyright © 1987 by Brenda Cole

ISBN: 0-373-06226-5

First Silhouette Books printing March 1987

America's Publisher of Contemporary Romance

Printed in the U.S.A.

RL 4.4, IL age 10 and up

First Love from Silhouette by Brenda Cole

BRENDA COLE was born and grew up in rural Alabama, the setting for some of her novels. The third of four daughters, she lived for many years on a small farm. She graduated from Greensboro High School and went on to Livingston University for a degree in English Education. Subsequently, she taught English in junior and senior high schools. After her marriage, she traveled all over the country with her husband. They now live in San Jose, California.

Chapter One

Brittany tossed the oversize, blue chambray shirt onto the growing pile of discarded clothes and went back to her closet for another blouse. There had to be something decent in there, she thought as she thumbed through the long row of hangers.

She finally stopped at a hand-crocheted sweater of heavy cotton. If she exchanged her sandals for her new suede boots and tied her hair back with her apricot-and-cream-colored silk scarf, it would work fine.

Even though it was already June and the first Saturday of summer vacation, the cool San Francisco Bay area mornings were comfortable enough for sweaters and boots, and with any luck, she'd find something new to wear before the day got too warm.

She was just adding the finishing touches to her hair when she heard her father calling from downstairs. "Brittany, hurry up! Your breakfast is on the table!"

"I'm coming, Dad," she called back and picked up her purse from the dresser. At the door, she paused and looked back at the room.

The bed was unmade, the closet door and three dresser drawers were open, and all the outfits she had rejected still cluttered the floor, but she didn't have time to straighten it at the moment.

Later, she promised herself, as she hurried down the stairs to the kitchen. Right after breakfast, she'd come back up here and take care of it.

The kitchen was heavy with the tangy aroma of fried bacon, and her father was already at the table when she slid into her seat beside him. She took one look at the crisp bacon and plump, golden French toast and pushed the plate away.

"Dad, I told you that I was going to start cutting down on calories. Now that school's out, I just want juice and toast for breakfast."

"So? That's what I fixed for you—toast."

"Very funny," she said, reaching for a piece of plain toast from a plate in the center of the table. "If I ate like that every day, I'd have to let out the strings of my bikini."

Frank Allen's eyebrows drew together over the bridge of his nose, and he fixed his daughter with a stern glare. "You'd better not let me catch you wearing anything that's held together with strings."

"I was just kidding. Between you and Nana, it's a wonder that I'm allowed to wear anything that shows my knees or elbows."

"That's not true. Your grandmother may be a little old-fashioned, but she doesn't complain about what you wear."

"I know," Brittany conceded, "and I do have Aunt Cecelia on my side. At least she knows something about fashion and style."

"Is she going shopping with you today?"

"No, I'm going with Mary Ann and Linda. We thought we'd start at Bryant Plaza and work our way back to Cordova Mall."

"What about money? Do you have enough?"

"I still have all my birthday money, but since you've brought up the subject, I could use a little something extra for gas." Before her father could object, she added, "I need all my money for clothes. I don't have anything new for summer."

"But why do you always have to drive when you go off with your girlfriends?"

"Linda and Mary Ann have to drive their parents' cars. I'm the only one with a car of my own."

"Maybe I should have thought about that before I let your aunts and uncles talk me into letting them buy you that car for Christmas. I just never thought I'd go broke putting gasoline in it."

"I thought you said that you felt better when you knew I was driving. You know I'm a good driver."

"Yes, but couldn't the other girls help out with the gas money occasionally?"

"They're not being cheap; they just don't think about it. Gasoline is usually someone else's problem."

"It just seems that ever since you got the car, you're always asking for gas money."

"If you let me have my own credit card, I wouldn't have to bother you."

"You can forget about that, I might complain, but at least this way I have some control over how much you spend."

Mr. Allen took out his wallet, thumbed through the bills and put it back. "I don't have any extra cash right now. Can you make it to your Uncle Ed's service station?"

"Sure. No problem."

"Tell him I said to fill it up and put it on my bill."

Her father had finished breakfast, and as he started for the living room, he pulled his keys out of his pocket.

Brittany was following him, but she hung back when he stopped to unlock the desk drawer and take out his police revolver.

Brittany's mother had been a member of the police department until she'd been killed by a stray bullet. For a long time after that, Brittany hadn't been able to stand the sight of a gun. Her father had taken to leaving his at the police station or in his squad car, but that was over ten years ago, and as he was still a policeman, Brittany had eventually had to accept guns as part of his life.

At least now that he had been promoted to detective, he didn't have to wear a uniform. With the gun concealed by his sports jacket, he looked just like any other father off to a day at the office. Brittany moved over to the door and waited for his goodbye kiss.

"Go over your day one more time for me," he said.

"First, I'm going to Uncle Ed's for gas, and then I'll pick up Mary Ann and Linda and head for the department stores. When we're through shopping, I'll take them home, and I'll go to Aunt Helen's."

"Are you going to stay there until I get home?"

"That depends. I have a date at seven, so I'll have to be back here by five so that I can get ready."

"I should be home by then, but I'll call you at Helen's if you're not here when I get in."

"Okay."

"And you know how to reach me if you need me?"

"Dad, I'll be fine. You've been at the same station for years. The entire police force knows my car, and I have relatives on every corner of this town."

"I know, but it's too easy for everyone to assume that you're with someone else. I want to be sure that I know where you are." Mr. Allen bent to kiss his daughter's cheek. "Just leave the house alone. I don't want you spending your whole vacation taking care of it, so I told Louise to start coming in three times a week to clean. She'll be in today."

"Thanks, Dad, I'll see you this afternoon."

After her father had left, Brittany went back to her room for a final inspection of her appearance. Slim and leggy, with shoulder-length black hair, a smooth complexion and clear blue eyes, she was accustomed to attracting a certain amount of attention everywhere she went, and she never left the house looking less than her best.

After she was satisfied that her clothes, hair and makeup were just right, she locked up the house and took her car out of the garage.

Considering what the wind would do to her hair, she hesitated before deciding to put the top down. After all, she reasoned, she was dressed warmly enough, and she loved the light-headed sense of freedom she got with the wind whipping around her.

Her uncle's service station wasn't very far away, but to get there, Brittany had to take one of the main freeways that was normally bumper-to-bumper with commuter traffic. Fortunately, the traffic wasn't as heavy on Saturdays, and she made it without any trouble.

Then her luck ran out. The line of cars parked at the full-service gasoline tanks stretched all the way to the street. She couldn't stop with the tail of her car still in the traffic, so she pulled around the line and parked at the self-service island.

One of her cousins, Billy Allen, was busy pumping gas, but when he saw her, he waved and raised his voice over the noise of the motors. "Troy's inside," he said about his brother. "Tell him to get out here and take care of your car."

"Thanks, I will," she answered, getting out of her car and stepping carefully around the various pools of oil and gasoline that puddled the pavement between her car and the office.

She opened the door and saw Troy and his best friend, Dave Walker, poring over some kind of brochure that they had spread out on her uncle's desk.

"Good morning," she called out to them.

Both boys looked up, but seeing it was only his cousin, Troy mumbled a greeting and turned back to the paper.

"Excuse me, but...uh...I need some gas," she said.

"Tell Billy," Troy said. "I'm not working here this summer."

"Billy's busy, and there's a long line at the full-service pumps, so I'm at the self-service..."

"Then do it yourself. That's what *self-service* means, you know."

"I don't know how."

"Then you should have gotten in line and waited your turn like everybody else."

Just then, Ed Allen walked in. "Get out there and fill up Brittany's car," he ordered.

Dave was already moving toward the door. "I'll do it," he said.

He stopped beside Brittany and held out his hand. "I need your keys."

Brittany looked confused, and he explained without her having to ask. "Your car has a lock on the gas tank, remember?"

"I'd almost forgotten." She laughed. "How did you know?"

"I helped Ed put it on," he said, letting the door slam behind him.

Ed's voice and manner softened perceptibly when he spoke to his niece. "Where are you headed so early in the morning?" he asked.

"Shopping." Brittany smiled. "Where else?"

"Is someone going with you?"

"Yes, and don't worry. I'll be all right. But if you want to do something for me, you'll let me charge my gas. Dad said I could put it on his bill. Is that all right?"

"You know it is."

"That's not fair," Troy said. "You have five nephews, and you never let any of us charge anything."

"But Brittany's my only niece. Besides, all you boys who are old enough to drive have jobs."

Someone called him from the garage area of the station, and Ed reached for the door, pausing long enough to say, "Take what you need, sweetheart, and if Troy gives you a hard time, tell Dave. He'll take care of you."

Brittany nodded and smiled at her uncle. When he left, she turned to Troy. "What did you mean when you said you weren't working here?" Brittany asked when her uncle left.

"I'm not. I'm going to be a camp counselor this summer."

"You? A counselor? Where?"

Troy picked up the brochure and held it up for her to see. "Camp Chabewa."

"What kind of place is that?"

"It's the summer camp I went to when I was nine and ten years old. Dave's been a counselor there for the past two summers, and he talked me into going with him this year."

"But how did you get them to hire you?"

"Dave's aunt and uncle own the place. He got them to give me the job."

Dave came back from filling up Brittany's gas tank. He held the keys out to her but kept the ring deep in his hand so that her fingertips brushed against his palm as she retrieved them.

"I hope you know what you're doing," she said teasingly.

Dave flushed. "What do you mean?" he asked.

"Getting Troy a job as a counselor, of course. If you ask me, he still needs someone to look after him."

"Oh, *that*." Dave shrugged. "It's not exactly what you would call hard work. We have campfires, go canoeing, hiking, fishing and swimming—things like that."

"How did it get a name like *Chabewa*? Is it Indian or something?"

"That's what the kids like to think—" Dave grinned "—but it's really just a contraction of my aunt's and uncle's names. Charles and Betty Walker."

"Cha...be...wa. I get it," she said. "It sounds like a lot of fun. Too bad they don't let girls go there, too."

"They do. It's a coed camp."

"Really? Do they need any girl counselors?"

"I don't know, but I could check on it for you if you want me to," he said.

"Sure, why not? It might be fun."

"Oh, Brittany, get serious!" Troy said. "The camp is out in the middle of nowhere. There isn't a single beauty parlor for miles. What would you do if you broke a fingernail?"

Brittany made a face at her cousin. "Haven't you heard? There are some wonderful false fingernails on the market now. They look so real you can hardly tell them from the real thing. I'll just bring a big supply of them with me."

"She's got you there!" Dave laughed.

He reached over and took the brochure out of Troy's hands and handed it to Brittany. "Look this over and then check it out with your father. If you think you'd want to be a counselor, I'll put in a good word for you."

"Why, thanks, Dave. I'll think about it," she said, putting the brochure away in her purse.

At the door, she looked back at Troy and smiled, "Wouldn't we have fun at camp together?"

"Oh, yeah, just wonderful."

As soon as she left, he turned on his friend. "Why did you do that? Do you think I want her tagging along with me all summer?"

"To tell you the truth, I wasn't thinking of *you*," Dave said.

"Then why..." he started but stopped himself when he saw the look on Dave's face. "Oh, no! Not you too!"

David dragged his eyes away from the sports car that was already disappearing in the morning traffic and looked back at Troy. "Me too, what?"

"You know what I mean. I've seen too many boys hanging around my spoiled cousin not to recognize the symptoms. I guess I missed the warning signs with you because I thought you were too smart to be caught."

"Maybe if you weren't her cousin, you could see what the rest of us do."

"Well, as her cousin, let me warn you not to get your hopes too high. She only talked about becoming a counselor to bug me. She won't do anything about it."

"How do you know?"

"Brittany has never had any kind of job—not even baby-sitting. Heck, she wouldn't even go to camp when she was younger because I told her that she'd have to make her own bed."

Dave refused to be deterred. "I'll bet you could get her to come to camp if you wanted to."

"I probably could, but I'm not going to."

"Remember when I set you up with that date with Linda Hooper, and you said that if there was ever anything you could do for me?" Dave asked.

"Yeah, but..."

"And I let you borrow my car last Friday night and didn't even charge you for the gas you used."

"Oh, come on now! Are you saying that if I get Brittany to come to camp, you'll call us even?"

"If you get her to come, I'll owe you," Dave said.

"What do you think it will accomplish?"

"Probably nothing," his friend admitted. "Except that I could see more of her than I do now."

"You'll find out that I've been right about her all along."

"I'm willing to take that chance."

"All right, then. If that's what you really want, come to Grandma's for lunch tomorrow. Brittany'll be there, and I'll see what I can do."

Chapter Two

Spending Sunday at her grandparents' house had been part of Brittany's life for as long as she could remember. When her mother was alive, they had alternated visits, spending one Sunday with Nana and Aunt Cecelia (her mother's family) and the next with Granny and Pap Allen and all her father's brothers and their families, but since the tragedy, the two sides had blended into one large family. Now, Nana and Aunt Cecelia came to the Allen's house every Sunday, also.

Except for special occasions, the weekly gatherings were loosely structured, and every family operated on its own schedule. Some came early and stayed late, and others just dropped in for lunch. Today, Brittany and her father had attended late mass and were the last to arrive.

Dave had been watching the door for the past hour, but when Brittany walked in, he hung back with Troy while everyone else gathered to welcome the latecomers.

"I hope we didn't hold up lunch," Frank said. "One of Brittany's boyfriends stopped us outside church, and I didn't think we were ever going to get away from him."

Brittany was going around the room hugging her grandparents, aunts and uncles, but she paused to protest. "He wasn't a boyfriend. He was just a friend."

"She's too young for a boyfriend," Nana insisted.

"I'm sure the boys wouldn't agree with you," her Aunt Ernestine interjected, "but I'm against her singling out any one boy for special attention."

"That's right," Aunt Helen agreed. "There's plenty of time for steady dating."

Aunt Cecilia stepped in and changed the subject. "Is that one of the new outfits you bought yesterday?" she asked.

"This old thing?" Brittany laughed. "Hardly. I bought one new dress yesterday, but I can't wear it until it's hemmed."

"Bring it over to me tomorrow and I'll do it for you," Nana said.

Troy was accustomed to the way they fussed over Brittany, and after a cursory glance in her direction, he turned back to the baseball game on television.

Dave, he noticed, was still staring at his cousin, and he poked him in the ribs.

"Close your mouth before you start drooling," he whispered.

Embarrassed, Dave pushed him back harder than necessary. "Have you done anything about getting her to come up to Blue Lake as a counselor?" he asked.

"Give me a chance! You just mentioned it yesterday."

"I know, but Aunt Betty and Uncle Charles have already filled most of the positions. I just wanted to make sure there's a spot for her."

"Hey, brat!" Troy called. "Did you hear that?"

"Don't call me brat," Brittany responded automatically and began making her way over to the sofa where Troy and Dave were sitting a little apart from the others. "Hear what?" she asked.

"Dave told his uncle to save a counselor's position for you. They've already turned down three other people."

Brittany's eyes widened, and she looked at Dave in dismay. "Oh, you didn't, did you? I mean, I was just—"

Troy poked Dave in the ribs again. "See? What did I tell you? That talk about becoming a counselor was just hot air."

"No, it wasn't. I just haven't had time to think about it. If…"

"Hey, don't worry about it. You couldn't handle a job like that, anyway," Troy said.

"What's that supposed to mean?"

"It's work, Brittany. The Walkers aren't paying us to do nothing. Besides taking care of the kids, the counselors have to work, too."

"It's not all that bad," Dave protested.

"It couldn't be, or Troy wouldn't be interested," Brittany said.

"Yeah? Well, don't forget I've already been hired. You know you couldn't handle it, so you won't even try."

"I can if you can."

"You'd be crying to come home before the first week was out."

"I would not!"

"Prove it," he dared.

Brittany looked over at Dave. "Did you really tell your aunt and uncle to save me a place?"

"No, Troy made that up, but I'm sure there are still a couple of openings for junior counselors. Are you interested?"

"You bet I am. It seems that I have something to prove to my cousin."

Helen Allen, Troy's mother, appeared in the doorway and announced that lunch was ready. Troy stood and leaned over to his cousin. "Hadn't you better check it out with Uncle Frank first? He may not let you go."

"Don't worry about Dad. I know how to handle him" was the answer.

The difficult part was going to be getting everyone else to agree. She was the only person alive who had a roomful of parents, and they all expected to be consulted about every aspect of her life.

Usually, she appreciated all the attention, but there were times when it created problems. The entire family discussed her allowance, how much makeup she could wear and even her choice of friends. Her first date had been the subject of many intense family meetings.

Since Dave needed an answer right away, Brittany decided that she might as well bring it up now. At the first lull in the conversation, she took a deep breath and asked, "Is it all right if I apply for a job as a counselor at Camp Chabewa this summer?"

There was a moment of stunned silence, and then her grandfather turned to Frank. "Why haven't you told us anything about this?" he demanded.

"It's the first I've heard of it," Frank said.

"I've been talking to Troy and Dave about it. I just made up my mind that I want to do it," Brittany said.

"What camp are you talking about?" Ernestine asked.

"It's the same one that Billy and Troy went to when they were younger. Dave's aunt and uncle run it," Helen said.

"You mean Charles Walker? The coach at Oak Grove High School?" Frank asked.

Dave nodded. "Yes, and my Aunt Betty is the school nurse there. They've been operating a camp up at Blue Lake for kids from nine to twelve during the summer for the past twelve or so years."

Ernestine glared at Dave, and her husband, Fred, said, "Blue Lake's over four hours from here. Brittany would have to stay overnight."

"How long were you planning to work there?" her father asked.

"I don't know. I haven't talked to Mr. and Mrs. Walker yet."

"Some of the counselors stay for the entire six weeks, but some just stay for a week," Dave said.

Cecilia laid her hand on Brittany's arm. "You haven't had any experience as a camp counselor. How would you know what to do?"

"It's not hard to learn the routine," Dave said. "All the new trainees are paired with experienced counselors."

"They must have some adults there," Frank said. "The whole camp can't be run by teenagers."

"Oh, no," David said. "Besides my aunt and uncle, there are two other married couples, and about half of the twenty counselors are college students. Uncle Charles says he gets senior counselors by bringing in new people every year and training them."

"I don't think it's a good idea for Brittany to even apply for a job like that until we have a chance to look into it more closely," Nana said.

"But I have to know right away. It starts next weekend," Brittany protested.

"Maybe next year, then," her father said. "That will give us more time to think about it."

Brittany sighed. "I was afraid you were going to say that. I told Linda that I'd probably wind up spending my summer here. At least we have something different to do this year."

"What's that?" Granny Allen asked.

"Linda's father is going to be a guest professor at the junior college this summer, and she said we could get an unlimited pass to the college swimming pool. A lot of good-looking guys hang out around there."

Troy choked on a mouthful of food, but no one seemed to notice. They all stared at Brittany in open-mouthed amazement.

Finally, Helen broke the silence. "Well, you know...Troy's going to be a counselor there this summer," she said. "He could keep an eye on Brittany."

"And Dave said that she didn't have to stay all summer. She could come home if she wanted to," Fred added.

Although the subject was reopened, it wasn't settled before lunch was over. Brittany knew they would make a number of telephone calls and cross-examine everyone they knew who had attended the camp. But at least she was given permission to fill out an application.

Dave just happened to have one with him, and despite Troy's constant interruptions, he helped her fill it out.

"Do you think I'll be accepted?" Brittany asked. "I don't have any experience, and I'm not good at sports or..."

"You have as good a chance as anyone else," Dave said.

"And better than most," Troy mumbled before Dave cut him off.

Dave looked over at the discussion still going on among the adults, and asked, "What about them? Are they going to let you go?"

"If they don't, I'll tell them about Mary Ann's idea of going on a hundred-mile bike-a-thon with a group from her hiking club," Brittany said.

Dave grinned and shook his head. "You really do know how to handle them, don't you?"

"When you have as many parents as I do, you have to be creative sometimes."

Dave tucked the application in his back pocket. "Aunt Betty will call you to set up a personal interview and go over everything with you, but I'll put in a good word for you," he said.

"Thanks," Brittany said. "I really want to show my dear cousin that I can do anything that he can."

Before she got out of bed the next morning, Dave called with the news. There was a problem with a broken water line and his aunt and uncle had had to rush back to the campgrounds. They wouldn't be able to hold any more interviews.

"I guess that means I don't get the job," Brittany said.

"No, it means that you already have the job."

"But how? I don't understand."

"To tell you the truth, they were in a bind. One of the counselors they've already hired can't start until week after next, and since they can't interview anyone else, I told them I would vouch for you. They said you could fill in for the first week, and if you worked out, maybe..."

"One week will be fine," Brittany assured him. "What should I do now?"

"Just pack whatever you're going to need and meet us in Oak Grove High School's parking lot Saturday morning."

Luckily, she hadn't thrown away the brochure that he had given her. During the next few days, she studied the colorful pictures of children swimming, climbing over rocks and singing around a campfire. Just watching a bunch of kids playing in the woods couldn't be as difficult as deciding what to pack, she thought.

After settling on which outfits to take with her, she still had to find matching shoes, coordinate her accessories and make room for all of the other necessities—makeup, hair dryer, hot rollers and mirrors. She managed to get everything into four suitcases, leaving the back seat of her car free for her new sleeping bag and air mattress.

The last thing she did on Friday was visit each of her relatives, picking up freshly baked cookies, extra spending money and advice along the way. She wanted to make sure they wouldn't come to see her off the next morning. It would be impossible to make a good first impression on Mr. and Mrs. Walker with her own relatives making more of a fuss than any of the children's.

She didn't know what she had missed by skipping the personal interview until she arrived at the school parking lot the next morning and realized that she didn't have the foggiest idea of what she was supposed to do.

The scene in front of her seemed to be one of utter confusion. Kids of every size rushed around dragging their suitcases and shouting to one another and their parents. No one seemed to be in charge, and for the first time since she had taken Troy's dare, Brittany began to have serious doubts. Maybe this wasn't for her, after all.

A familiar voice called her name, and she looked up to see Dave coming toward her.

"Thank heavens you're here. I was beginning to feel a little overwhelmed," she said.

"Yeah, well, it's usually like this on the first and last days. Everyone gets kind of excited."

"So I see."

"You want to come over and meet my aunt and uncle before we load your stuff on the bus?"

"On the bus? Why can't I just leave it in my car?"

"We all go to the camp on buses."

Brittany looked at the hulking yellow vehicles and wrinkled her nose. "Do we have to? They look so hot and . . . bumpy."

"That's half the fun. It makes you glad to get off when we get to Blue Lake."

"I don't doubt that," she said, her voice barely reaching him as they worked their way through the noisy crowd to a small booth where Mr. and Mrs. Walker were checking off each new arrival.

"Uncle Charles, Aunt Betty, this is Brittany Allen," Dave said.

"Call me Coach," Charles Walker said shaking her hand.

"And me, Betty, or Miss Betty if you feel more comfortable," his wife added.

"Thank you. I appreciate you giving me this chance, especially since I've never done anything like this before," Brittany said.

Coach's eyes twinkled. "You came highly recommended," he said, before he walked off to talk to one of the bus drivers.

A young woman leading a small, pale boy by the hand, interrupted them. "Mrs. Walker, I'm Rhonda Wayne, and I . . . uh, I have a problem."

"Oh?" Betty asked, sympathetically. "Maybe I can help."

"Sometimes Bobby gets carsick if he has to ride for any length of time, and he's afraid he'll embarrass himself in front of all the other children."

"Oh, dear," Betty said. "The bus is the only transportation we provide, but if you want to take him to camp yourself . . ."

"I can't," Mrs. Wayne said. "I'm supposed to be in a tennis tournament at two, and I can't get out of it."

Dave spoke up quickly. "Aunt Betty, Brittany has her car. She was planning to drive, anyway. I know she wouldn't mind driving Bobby if Mrs. Wayne approves.''

"I'll approve, I mean, as long as she's a counselor, and everything."

"She's a junior counselor, but I could ride along with them," Dave volunteered.

"The official transportation is by bus," Betty said, "but I have no objections to Bobby going by private car, as long as you sign a release."

Mrs. Wayne was already taking her pen out of her purse. "Oh, I'll sign it, all right," she said. "I've already given him some medication, so he *should* be all right. In fact, if you have a place for him to lie down, he'll probably sleep all the way there."

"I can fix him a bed in the back seat of my car," Brittany said and then smiled at Bobby. "I know exactly how you feel. I used to get carsick, too."

"Go ahead and get him set up," Dave told her. "After I finish helping getting the buses loaded, I'll join you."

After Mrs. Wayne gave her son several enthusiastic hugs and kisses, Brittany led him back to her car. She let him help her arrange the sleeping bag into a comfortable bed, and while she waited for Dave, he crawled in and stretched out.

Troy stopped by to ask if she needed any help getting her gear on the bus, but when he discovered she was taking her car, he walked away shaking his head.

Finally, after all the other campers and counselors had been absorbed by the buses and their parents had driven away, she saw Dave approaching. He caught her eye and raised the clipboard he was carrying.

"I'm sorry that took so long," he called. "Are you ready to roll?"

Brittany nodded and put her finger to her lips, pointing to the back seat. "Bobby's medication has already taken effect," she said.

"So I see." Dave grinned. "He looks as if he's going to have a comfortable ride to the camp."

"So will I, thanks to you," she said. "I hope you don't mind letting a girl drive for you."

"Not at all." He stretched out his legs and folded his arms across his chest. "You watch the road and I'll watch you."

"What?" she asked.

"Oh, nothing. Just a little joke," he said.

"I'm surprised that a friend of Troy's would feel comfortable with me driving."

"Why?"

"He has this crazy idea that I'm too spoiled to do anything for myself. I thought he might have warned you."

"Are you saying he's wrong?"

Brittany shrugged. "If being spoiled means wanting my own way or having people do things for me, then . . . I guess I am. But that doesn't mean I'm helpless. In spite of what Troy says."

Dave chuckled. "Do you two fight all the time?"

Brittany smiled. "Pretty much, I guess."

"It obviously doesn't bother you."

"Sometimes it does, but I'd never let him know it. He might stop."

"And you don't want him to?"

Brittany hesitated. "If you ever tell him I said it, I'll deny it, but I need him just the way he is. I know I can trust him not to pull any punches. That's why I have to show him that I can survive a week at this job without any special help."

"If there's anything I can do for you, just let me know."

"That's the whole point, remember? Without any help."

"Then I'll do whatever I can to make it harder for you."

Brittany laughed. "You don't have to go that far."

Because they were following the string of buses, Brittany didn't have to concentrate on where she was going, and with Dave to keep her entertained, she didn't realize how far they had traveled until the highway began to climb higher into the Sierra foothills.

Chapter Three

When they turned off the main highway a few miles north of Kings Canyon National Park, the road began to wind deeper into the forest. The trees lining the highway grew so tall that they seemed to touch overhead, effectively blocking out the sun in some places.

"How much farther is it?" Brittany asked, as she followed the buses onto an unpaved road.

"A few more miles. Just around the next bend," Dave said.

The last portion of the trip was the most difficult. It took all her attention and skill as a driver to keep the car from sliding on the loose gravel or hitting a washed-out place in the road.

The sudden change in the ride woke Bobby, but Dave managed to keep him distracted so that he wouldn't think about the bouncing of the car until Brittany finally brought it to a stop inside the main gates of Camp Chabewa.

"Those last few miles were pure torture," she said, climbing out of the car and stretching.

"Yeah, but aren't you glad you're here," Dave said.

Brittany looked around her. Her image of charming little log cabins nestled beneath the trees dissolved into the dust and dirt surrounding several plain, strictly utilitarian buildings and weather-beaten bleachers that circled a long flagpole. Even the flag seemed limp and uninspired.

The doors of the buses opened, and the children began pouring out. As soon as they were handed their bags, they ran off in different directions.

"Where are they going?" Brittany asked.

"To stow their gear in their cabins," Dave said. He looked down at his clipboard and added, "Bobby, you're in my cabin, B1. It's the first boys' cabin on your right. Brittany, you're in G4, the next to the last cabin just over the crest of that hill."

Bobby ran off to get his bag from the bus, but Brittany stood still, waiting.

"Is something wrong?" Dave asked.

"I was wondering who's supposed to help us with our luggage."

Dave started to laugh and then realized she was serious. "We have to take care of that ourselves," he said gently.

"But that's crazy! It'll take me all day to get my things up that hill."

She unlocked the trunk of her car, and when he saw all her luggage, he whistled. "Someone should have told you to pack just one bag."

"I don't know why. I couldn't possibly have gotten everything I needed in one bag."

"That's all right." He sighed. "I'll just have to help you."

Brittany didn't hear him. She'd spotted a group of male counselors standing around the buses. Since they weren't doing anything else, she was sure they wouldn't mind helping her.

"Excuse me." She smiled. "Could any of you help me..."

"Sure! I can! What do you need?" came the expected chorus of replies.

"Some help getting my things up to my cabin."

One especially good-looking counselor, slightly taller than the others and very striking looking with black hair and attractive dark eyes, stepped forward. "The rest of you go on about your business. I'll help this little lady."

Brittany returned his warm smile with one of her own. "Thanks, but this lady has four 'not-so-little' suitcases."

His eyebrows shot up, but he didn't falter. He put his arms around the two boys standing beside him. "I was wrong, boys. This is going to take all of us."

"I'm sorry to be so much trouble," she said, letting her eyes touch all three boys as she included them in her laughing apology. "I'm Brittany Allen, and in case you haven't guessed, this is the first time I've ever been to camp."

"That gives us something in common. I'm Sean McCashen, and this is my first year, too."

"I'm Bill Howland. This is my second year as a counselor, but it's my brother George's first year," Bill said, introducing himself and his brother.

They walked back to her car, and Brittany gestured toward the luggage that Dave had unloaded from the trunk. "See what I mean," she said.

"At least you've already recruited Dave," Bill said, shaking hands with Dave and introducing him to the other boys before picking up one of Brittany's suitcases.

Sean held back until all the suitcases were taken and then hoisted Brittany's sleeping bag onto his shoulder and fell into step with her. "Why did you and Dave come up in a separate car?" he asked. "Is there something going on between you that the rest of us should know about?"

"Of course not," she replied quickly. "One of the campers couldn't ride the bus, so I brought him, and Dave just came along to show me the way."

"This may be my first time here, but I think I could have managed to follow the buses," Sean commented dryly.

Ahead of them, Dave stopped the string of boys at a fork in the path and looked back over his shoulder at Brittany. "There's your cabin. Boys aren't allowed over there, so we'll leave your things here."

"Thanks, to all of you," she said, and then lowered her voice so that only Dave could hear. "What do I do now?"

"Just go on in and get settled. Your cabin mate should be along shortly. She'll help you out from there."

"I hope so. I'm beginning to suspect that Troy was right after all. I may be out of my element here."

"You've only been here a few minutes," he reminded her. "Give it a chance."

Brittany looked at the cabin. There was certainly nothing encouraging about its appearance. It was a plain, rectangular building with two small windows on each side and a door at either end. The windows were positioned so close to the ceiling that curtains, or any other kind of covering, were unnecessary.

She picked up her sleeping bag and walked over and pushed opened the door. Inside, there were four bunk beds lined up along the wall and two single cots, one at either end of the room. There was no other furniture or any decorations to relieve its severity.

A sudden movement caught her eye, and she looked up to see a group of girls staring down at her from one of the top bunks. One of them asked, "All all those boys your boyfriends?"

"Of course not," she said nervously. "They were just helping me with my luggage."

"The one with black hair looks like a movie star," a pudgy little girl in a red jump suit declared.

"I like the one who was in front. He helped me get checked in this morning, and he's nice," another girl insisted, prompting the rest of the girls to voice their own opinions as they climbed down from the beds.

"Who left all this gear out here?" an authoritative voice called to them from outside.

The slim girl standing there was about her own age with medium-length brown hair, green eyes and a light sprinkling of freckles across the bridge of her nose. In her faded cutoffs and loose T-shirt, she looked right at home.

"I'm sorry," Brittany said. "It's mine. I just haven't had a chance to bring it inside."

"You brought all this with you?"

Brittany noticed the single duffel bag slung over the girl's shoulder and the sleeping bag in her hand. "I know it looks like a lot, but it's all necessary."

"Okay, let's get it inside," she said. She turned away before Brittany could see her expression, but the strain in her voice was unmistakable. "By the way, I'm Jenny Kurk and, according to my chart, you must be Brittany Allen."

"Yes," Brittany answered, struggling with two suitcases and trying to push another one along with her foot.

Jenny picked up the other suitcase and put it beside one of the single beds and began shouting orders to the younger girls. "Each of you choose a bunkmate and a bed. Spread your sleeping bags on your bed and stow your gear under the bottom bunk."

There was an eager scuffle as the little girls rushed around following instructions. Brittany watched for a moment and then pulled over one of her suitcases and started taking out her things.

Suddenly she stopped and looked around. "Jenny, where are the closets? I need to hang..."

"There aren't any. Everything has to stay in your suitcase under the bed."

"But that's impossible. I can't get all my things under there, and even if I could, they would be too wrinkled to wear. I'll just have to hang some of them...in the...bathroom."

Her voice trailed off as she looked all around.

"It's outside and down the path. We share a bathroom with fifty other girls," Jenny said.

Brittany clamped her lips together and closed the suitcase. She'd prepared herself to accept primitive conditions such as no air conditioning, television or telephones, but outdoor plumbing was going too far. Furthermore, she didn't enjoy looking like an idiot in front of the younger girls.

Silently, she spread her air mattress on the canvas-covered springs of her cot and was just beginning to inflate it when a shrill whistle broke the silence.

One of the girls jumped and gave a little scream and some of the others started giggling.

"That's just the camp whistle," Jenny said. "You'll get used to it."

"It means that lunch is ready," the pudgy little girl explained with an air of superiority. "Can we go on to the cafeteria now? I'm hungry."

"Just a second. Before anyone leaves, I need to check you off against my list and make sure that you're all in the right cabin."

"Marlene Lee. And Jada Williams," the first two girls called out as they lined up at the door.

They were followed in turn by Beth Fondren, Nettie Fretwell, Melba Deloach, Rebecca Slade, Judy Kimbrough and Pam Langham.

After Jenny finished checking them off, she said, "Since Marlene and Jada were here last year, they can lead the way. When you get to the cafeteria, I want all of us to sit together so that we can start getting to know each other."

She waited for the girls to file past and then fell into step with Brittany. "Are you all right?"

"I don't know. I'm beginning to wonder why I'm here."

"Why are you?"

"Because of a stupid dare. Since you got stuck with me for a cabin mate, you might as well know right now that I've never been to a camp in my whole life."

"I'd already figured that much out for myself," Jenny said, and then, because Brittany looked so miserable, added, "Don't worry. The great thing about camp is that you can kick back and do things you'd never do at home. Just relax. We'll manage."

Brittany wasn't so sure, but it sounded good and she wanted to believe it. Besides, right now she was hungry, and that took precedence over everything else.

The cafeteria was serving box lunches at the picnic tables. As soon as everyone was settled, Jenny began asking questions, effectively drawing out each of the little girls until Brittany began to recognize the separate and distinctive personalities that made up their group.

Marlene and Jada were longtime best friends, and because they had been at Camp Chabewa the year before, they were already establishing themselves as the cabin leaders.

Beth and her bunkmate, Nettie, had never met before, but they looked enough alike to be sisters. That, however, was as far as the resemblance went. While Beth was shy and said little, Nettie chattered constantly.

Judy and Rebecca were total opposites in appearance, one tall and angular with large thick-lensed glasses and the other cute and petite, but they were well matched in every other way.

The last two girls, Pam and Melba, were the oldest and only occasionally forgot their advanced age long enough to join the rest of the group in laughter.

Just as they were finishing their meal, Coach Walker gave a short, welcoming speech and introduced the other adult advisers, the Clarks and the Jacksons. Then he introduced each of the senior counselors and asked them to take their campers back to their cabins for orientation while he met with the junior counselors.

Jenny stood up and began gathering her trash and instructing the girls to do the same. "Hurry up now. We have a lot of things to cover before we can have some free time," she said.

"What about me?" Brittany asked.

"Relax. Coach is just going over some of the basic rules with all of you. You can meet me back in the cabin when he finishes."

Jenny led the girls away, and Brittany moved closer to the front and took a seat at an empty table.

She wasn't alone for long. Sean joined her saying, "I guess this is where we learn all the dos and don'ts."

"I hope so," she said, her spirits buoyed by the appreciative glint in his eye.

The other junior counselors moved up and filled in the other seats around Coach. He took a few minutes to introduce them all, but Brittany had already met so many people that day that all their names ran together. She was glad when he concluded the introductions and distributed a small handbook of the rules and regulations.

"Whether you are a returning junior counselor or a rookie, I want each one of you to study these rules," he said. "You all have a senior counselor in your cabin, but you can't expect to lean on him or her for all the answers. I'm not going to excuse any infraction just because you didn't know the rule."

Brittany started thumbing through her book, and then realized that Coach was still talking. Quickly, she directed her attention back to him.

"One of the things that we are very strict about is that one counselor must be with the children whenever they are in their cabins—during the rest period immediately after lunch and, of course, after curfew. On alternate nights, or whatever you work out with your cabin mate, you can have a few free hours to stay out later, but all the children must be inside their cabin by nine o'clock.''

He didn't cover all the rules in detail, but he explained how the daily maintenance of the camp was shared by each cabin taking responsibility for a different job each day.

"Even though the campers are expected to help, you counselors are ultimately responsible to see that the work is done correctly. Just to make it more interesting, we have included the way your chores are done as part of the Best Cabin contest. In addition to how well your cabin does its chores, you can earn points or get demerits for punctuality, attitude and skill on the recreational field, and of course, the scavenger hunt, but you'll learn more about that tonight.''

In closing, he added, "All of you were given your work assignments in the personal interview, but if you need to check with me about anything, you can see me now.''

As soon as Brittany stood up, Sean did, too. "I'll walk you back to your cabin,'' he said.

"Thanks, but I have to see Coach about my assignment. What's yours?''

"Teaching archery,'' he said with a wink. "Are you interested in some private lessons?''

"We'll see.'' She was smiling as she walked away to find Coach. He was talking to the Howland brothers, so she waited until he acknowledged her.

"I'll bet you're curious about your job,'' he said.

"Well, yes, a little.''

"We've decided to try you out in first aid."

"Really?"

"According to your application, you've had two first-aid courses, so that makes you qualified. Come on over to the infirmary after the next whistle, and Betty will fill you in on the details."

Brittany turned to leave and saw Troy waiting for her.

"How are you making out?" he asked, falling into step with her.

"All right, I guess. I have a really nice cabin mate. How about you?"

"I'm bunking with Dave."

"I should have guessed."

When they reached the path to her cabin, Troy left Brittany with a reminder. "Let me know when you're ready to back out."

"Don't hold your breath," she called after him.

There was a flutter of activity from her cabin, and Brittany looked up in time to see the girls peeping out the window and waved at them.

"Is *he* your boyfriend?" Pam asked her as soon as she stepped inside."

"No—" she laughed "—he's definitely not my boyfriend."

Jenny was unabashedly watching Troy walk away. "Why not?" she asked. "He's cute and with your looks, I'll bet you could..."

"He's my cousin."

"Oh?" Jenny grinned widely. "That's even better."

"Now that you've brought it up, there really are some good-looking guys here," Brittany said. "Don't you think that Sean is handsome?"

"No, from what I could tell, he's too flashy. The one you should meet is Dave," Jenny said.

"You mean Dave Walker?"

"Oh, that's right—you and he came up together in your car. After the fuss that Glenda made, I don't know how I could have forgotten it."

"Who's Glenda?" Brittany asked.

"One of the other counselors. She and Dave went together some last summer, and I'm pretty sure she planned to pick up where they left off."

"Well, she doesn't have anything to worry about from me. Dave is Troy's best friend, and I've known him for years. There's nothing between us."

"Why not? Don't you think he's cute?"

Brittany thought of Dave's short cropped blond hair, his nice hazel eyes and friendly smile. She shrugged. "I guess so. I just never thought about it before. He's always been like another cousin."

"With a cousin like Troy, you don't need any others," Jenny said.

Brittany's reply was cut off by the whistle. This time there were no screams, but Jenny explained, anyway.

"That means the rest period is over. Normally, we'd go to the recreational field for some kind of organized games or relay races and then have a little free time, but today is more informal. We can do pretty much as we please, as long as we keep an eye on the kids."

"What are you going to do?" Brittany asked.

"Probably go down to the pier. That's usually where we all hang out when we're not busy. Want to come?"

"I can't right now. I have to go see Miss Betty at the infirmary. She's going to tell me what I have to do in first aid."

"When you finish, just follow the noise to the lake," Jenny said.

Chapter Four

The infirmary was actually the back room of Coach and Betty's summer house, and besides serving as the first-aid station, it was also the general office.

The heavy wooden door was open and through the screen door, Brittany could see Betty sitting at the desk. She knocked lightly, and Betty looked up and smiled.

"Come on in," she said. "I see that Charles has given you your assignment."

"Yes, but I have to confess—it was my father's idea that I take those first-aid courses. I've never used my training."

"That's all right. I'm a registered nurse, and Mrs. Clark has had paramedic training, so you won't be called on to do anything more serious than apply a Band-Aid. In fact, I don't want you taking it on yourself to do more than that unless we give you specific instructions."

"That's a relief. I was beginning to wonder if I could handle the job."

"Basically, we need you so that we can always have someone on duty. When Mrs. Clark or I can't be here, you'll be in charge. Of course we both have beepers, so if there's an emergency, you can always reach one of us," Betty explained.

"I think I can handle that."

"The most important thing for you to remember is that everything we do must be written down on this chart. Every child who takes any kind of medication, including vitamins, is listed on the master chart on the wall. If someone comes in when you're here alone, double-check his name and dosage and then write it down."

Betty paused for a breath before finishing with "Do you have any questions?"

"Not really. Everything seems pretty clear," Brittany answered.

"Well, since I'm going to be here logging the rest of the medical information on the children, you can relax and get acquainted with the other counselors and the campgrounds. Report back here after breakfast tomorrow morning."

"Thanks." Brittany turned to leave but hesitated by the door until her ears got accustomed to the different sounds. Then she headed down the hill toward the lake. Kids of all shapes and sizes were splashing in the water, running around beneath the trees or just stretched out on the grass.

She spotted Jenny sitting with Troy and Dave, and the other junior counselors on the pier and hurried over to join them.

"Did you get checked out in the infirmary?" Jenny asked.

Brittany gave a self-effacing smile. "Basically, I learned that I'm not supposed to do anything but sit by the paging system and call someone for help."

"You should be good at doing nothing," Troy said. "I'd hate to think you were in charge of anyone's health and safety."

Glenda, a pretty counselor with short, curly, caramel-colored hair was sitting between Dave and Troy, and she gave Troy an affectionate push. "That's not a very nice thing to say about Brittany, even if she is your cousin."

"I think it's a perfect job for Brittany," Sean said. "She can learn how to mend all the hearts she breaks."

Brittany felt her face growing warm. She wasn't sure how to handle such open flattery.

"Give us a break!" Bill Howland exclaimed. "You could at least hold off on the heavy-duty stuff until you get her alone."

"Oh, what would you know about it, anyway?" Sean flared.

"Maybe I should throw both of you in the water and cool you off," George suggested.

"I wouldn't, if I were you. It's not worth it," said one of the other counselors, still wearing a name tag that identified her as Sandy Cross.

"What do you mean?" George asked.

"If you get caught doing something like that, your cabin could lose as much as ten or fifteen points," Jenny explained.

"What's the big deal with the contest, anyway?" Sean asked.

Jenny said, "On the last night of camp, the boys' and girls' cabins with the most points are honored by the other cabins."

"There's a banquet and entertainment—all provided by the other cabins," Bill said. "My cabin won *once* last year."

"Is it hard to earn points?" Brittany asked.

"It's all spelled out in your handbook," Glenda told her.

"You earn the most points with the scavenger hunt," Dave explained. "Each cabin gets an identical list of fifty or so items, and you get so many points for each item that you find."

"That sounds easy enough," George said. "When does it start?"

"We should get the list tonight at the campfire. We'll have the rest of the week to find the things that are listed, but it's not as easy as it sounds. Last year we almost went crazy looking for a pair of knitting needles," Jenny said.

"Yeah, that's how we won. I just happened to find them taped to the underside of one of the picnic tables," Bill said.

"It sounds all right to me, but I can't help thinking that someone with the last name of *Walker* might have an unfair advantage over the rest of us," Sean said.

"That's not true," Dave said, "but if you have a problem with it, why don't you go talk to my aunt and uncle?"

To ease the tension that had suddenly developed, Jenny said, "I think I'll go for a swim. Brittany, do you want to go change and join me?"

"In there?" she asked doubtfully, looking at the churned-up lake.

"It's safe for swimming, but there's a swimming pool if you'd prefer."

Brittany automatically considered her hair. It was already after four o'clock, and if she went into the water now, she wouldn't have time to wash and dry it before dinner.

"I think I'll pass today. I just want to walk around and get to know the place. I didn't even know there was a swimming pool," Brittany said.

"I'll come with you," Sean said.

"Me too," George added.

Sean was already on his feet, and he looked down at George. "You weren't invited," he said meaningfully.

"I'll be the guide, and anyone who wants to come along can," Dave said.

"I do," Glenda said, stretching out her hand to Dave so that he could pull her up.

"Glenda, you were here last year. Don't tell me you've forgotten what the camp looks like," Jenny said, sharply.

As the little group started off, Sean stepped to Brittany's side, effectively cutting off George, but Brittany recognized his ploy and hesitated just long enough for George to move to her other side.

While Sean was the better looking of the two boys, George was cute, and she liked his easygoing manner. With the whole week ahead of her, Brittany wasn't ready to rule out either one of them just yet.

Dave led them along the lakeshore, pointing out the canoes and the boathouse, which held the fishing supplies and life preservers. There was also a trail that would take them around the lake.

"Can the counselors take the canoes out on the lake whenever they want to?" Sean asked.

"If you don't have anything else to do, and someone knows you're going," Dave said.

"How about it, Brittany?" Sean asked. "Would you like to go for a ride sometime?"

"Would I have to paddle?"

"Not if you went with me," George answered.

"Thanks, George." She laughed, trying to ignore the scowl on Sean's face. It wasn't going to be easy to keep things light and easy with Sean. He was obviously unaccustomed having to compete with anyone else for attention.

They left the lake and headed back toward the main campsite, passing the large, level field that Brittany had seen when they'd first arrived. Dave explained that it was the playing field, used for softball, volley-ball and other games and relay races.

"The boys' cabins are over there," he continued, pointing to a row of buildings that looked just like the girls' cabins, "and, of course, there's the swimming pool."

"Are you sure you wouldn't like to go swim-ming?" Sean asked. "I can't wait to see you in a swimming suit."

"They'll be blowing the whistle for dinner in a few minutes," Dave said quickly.

"I think I'd better go back to my cabin and finish getting my things..." Brittany caught herself before saying "put away" and substituted "organized." "I didn't finish before lunch."

"I'll walk with you," Sean said.

"That's all right," she said. "You'd have to walk all the way over the hill and then back."

"Then promise you'll sit with me at dinner," Sean said.

"According to the rule book, we have to sit with the people from our cabins," George pointed out.

"I'll see you later," Brittany promised, including both boys in her glance.

They watched her go and immediately stopped pre-tending they were interested in a tour. Glenda waited until they had wandered away before taking Dave's arm.

"It looks as if they're both trying to stake their claim on Brittany," she said. "I wonder who's going to win?"

"I wouldn't know," Dave said.

"At least they're lucky that they're all junior counselors."

"What has that got to do with anything?"

"Well, since you're a senior counselor this year, your off-duty nights will be the same as the college group's."

"I'm not the only high school student who's a senior counselor. There's Jenny."

"Yes, but wouldn't you rather be off with the junior counselors?"

Why hadn't he thought about that?

Unwinding his arm from Glenda's, Dave said, "Excuse me, but I have to see Troy about something."

"Now?" she asked.

"Yeah, I want to talk to him about trading nights with me," he answered as he hurried off.

Dave headed back to the pier but saw Troy and Jenny walking toward her cabin. That was a good sign. If Troy liked Jenny, it would be easy to get him to switch schedules.

He changed his direction and went to the crook in the path where Troy would have to turn to go back to his own cabin. He didn't have to wait very long.

Minutes later, Troy rounded the corner and came to an abrupt halt. "Who are you waiting to ambush?" he asked.

"You," Dave said, falling into step with him. "I wanted to ask you about switching off nights with me."

"Why?"

"Why do you think?"

"If it has something to do with my cousin, I've told you what I think. She's been twisting boys around her little finger since she was a baby. If you let her know how you feel, you'll be just like the rest of them."

"I've been hiding my feelings for years, and I can't see what it's gotten me. Most of the time she treats me as if I were part of the scenery."

"You think you'll be better off letting her walk all over you?"

"At least it would be a change. I don't want to go on like this, and I figure if I'm ever going to make a move, this is the week to do it. So—will you? Change nights with me, I mean? It'll only be for a week. After she leaves, we can change back, if you want to."

"What's in it for me?"

"It would put you on the same schedule with Jenny."

"I hadn't thought about that." Troy grinned. "I guess I could make the sacrifice."

They rounded up their campers, and then while Troy supervised the boys, Dave went to the cafeteria to help them set up for the wiener roast. By the time the dinner whistle blew, the bonfire was going well and there were plenty of sharpened sticks waiting for the hungry campers.

As busy as he was, Dave knew the very minute Brittany and Jenny showed up with their campers. He tried to catch her eye, but she was busy with the children and didn't even glance in his direction. He derived some comfort from the fact that she didn't pay any of the other male counselors any attention, either.

Actually, they had all they could handle just trying to keep their group of girls together and help them with their plates and hot dogs. It was amazing that out of the eight girls, not one of them could thread a frankfurter on a stick or spread mustard on a bun.

"I feel like the old woman who lived in a shoe." Brittany was commenting as she handed another hot dog to Pam.

"I know what you mean." Jenny laughed. "Just don't forget to get something to eat for yourself."

"After all this, I'm not hungry. I was hoping it might be getting close to bedtime."

"Not yet. We have to go to the bleachers at the flagpole for a closing ceremony around the campfire," Jenny said. "And since it's your night to turn in with the girls, you'd better eat now. This isn't like home; you can't raid the refrigerator at midnight."

Jenny's warning had its desired effect. Brittany took time to fix a plate for herself. By the time she finished eating, it was time to clean up their table and get over to the flagpole.

As one of the senior counselors blew "Taps", the flag was slowly lowered and Coach lit the campfire. The flames grew until they pushed back the gathering dusk, and Brittany realized that she had managed to survive one day, or most of it, anyway. Right now, home seemed so far away.

Coach had started talking, and with an effort, Brittany brought her mind back to him.

"Some of you have already been asking about our scavenger hunt, so before we get to the songs and stories that will wind up our first day, I'll distribute a list of items to the counselors. If the rest of you will pay attention, I'll read it aloud for you."

As he began to read through the list, a groan went up from the crowd. There were the usual things like a perfectly round rock, a bird feather, the longest piece of string and a comic book, but there were some strange things as well—a clothespin, a rubber duck, pink hair ribbons and the bonus item, a carefully hidden treasure chest full of jewels.

"It's only worth about a dollar ninety-eight cents," Coach said, "but the cabin that finds it will get twenty-five extra points."

After the excitement subsided, Coach turned the meeting over to Bob Clark who led them in some old folk songs and then told stories about some of the animals of the area, their habits and antics.

The stories were interesting and informative, as well as humorous, and they made Brittany eager for her first glance of a raccoon or deer. Finally, Mr. Jackson brought the evening to a close with a short devotional, and then Coach dismissed them.

"All of you get to the bathroom and back into the cabin as fast as you can," Jenny said. "The first cabin that gets their lights off wins two points, and anyone with their lights on when the last whistle blows, *loses* two points.''

"I'm supposed to go back with the girls tonight, and you'll come later, right?'' Brittany asked.

"Yes, but I won't be too far behind you. Just make sure that you get our lights off before the whistle blows,'' Jenny said.

Although Brittany stayed after the girls, hurrying them along, they weren't the first ones to get back to their cabin. However, they did get the lights off before the whistle.

Betty came around to check on each cabin, and as soon as she left, Marlene sat up in her bed and whispered, "Brittany? Is it all right if we tell ghost stories?''

Brittany hesitated. "I don't know.''

"Oh, please! Everyone at camp does it, and we won't turn on any lights or anything.''

"I don't want to hear any ghost stories,'' Beth said.

"I know one that's not really a ghost story. I heard it at camp last year, and it happened just a few miles from here,'' Jada said.

"Brittany, come over here with me,'' Beth said.

Brittany didn't want to hear the story any more than Beth did, but she couldn't let the younger girls know she was afraid, so she crept across the darkened room and climbed into Beth's bed while the rest of the girls gathered on the foot or the floor beside it.

Jada waited until everyone was quiet. Then she lowered her voice and spoke very slowly.

"Year before last, a man and a woman were going camping in the park near here, but they got lost and ended up on the road that comes out here. Anyway, they ran out of gas, and . . . well, you know there isn't a gas station or anything around here, so the man told his wife that he would go find some help. He told her to stay in the car and keep all the doors and windows locked until he got back."

Jada paused. There wasn't a single sound in the room, not even breathing, so she continued, "The man hadn't been gone but a little while when the woman felt something bump against the side of the car. She could hear a scraping noise, and she looked out, but it was too dark to see anything. The scraping got louder and louder, and at one time, she thought it was tapping out some kind of signal, but she remembered what her husband had said and didn't open the door. She just kept waiting, and when her husband didn't return, she finally went to sleep.

"When she woke up the next morning, a policeman was standing outside the car. He told her to get out but—not to look down. Of course, as soon as he said that, she looked. Then she knew what had been making the noises she had heard all night. It was her husband, and he had been . . ."

Just then, something struck the side of the cabin, and they all clutched at one another, too afraid to even scream.

Chapter Five

Brittany," a voice from outside called. "Are you in there?"

Brittany let out the breath she'd been holding. "It's all right. It's just Sean," she said.

She didn't have to say anything else. All eight girls scrambled to one of the top bunks on that side of the room.

"Come up here, Brittany," Marlene said. "You'll get in trouble if you go outside."

Brittany climbed up on the bunk and peered out into the darkness. She could see Sean standing in the shadows of one of the large trees.

"What are you doing here?" she asked.

"I want to talk to you. Can you come outside a minute?"

Jada tugged at her sleeve. "Don't go. If you get caught, you'll get in trouble."

"I can't," she called back, "and I don't think you should be out there, either."

"No, it's all right as long as I stay over here," he said. "I already checked."

"Why aren't you in your cabin?"

"My cabin mate's there. I just wanted to ask you about tomorrow."

Suddenly a light flickered across the path and focused on Sean. "Young man!" Mrs. Clark shouted. "You stay right there!"

"Quick! Duck!" one of the girls whispered, and instinctively Brittany obeyed. Crouched down on the bed, she could hear Mrs. Clark berating Sean.

"Boys are strictly forbidden over here! Since this is your first year, and it's only the first night, I'm only going to give you ten demerits. But if anything like this happens again, you'll be called up before Mr. Walker and dismissed!"

Inside the cabin, they couldn't hear Sean's reply, but there was no mistaking the loud knock at their door a moment later.

Before Brittany could climb down from the bunk to answer it, the door swung open, and Mrs. Clark waved her flashlight around the room.

"Just as I thought," she said when she saw them all crowded on the top bunks. "Were any of you talking to that boy outside?"

Brittany could feel the tension around her, and when she tried to speak, her words sounded strange to her own ears, "Yes ma'am. I did."

"Did you hear what I told him?" Mrs. Clark asked.

Brittany nodded.

"Well, the same goes for you. You get ten demerits and a warning. If this happens again, you could be sent home!"

Mrs. Clark left and slammed the door after her.

"Why did you tell her you were talking to him? We lost ten whole points!" Melba complained.

"I had to. I couldn't—"

"No, you didn't," Nettie interrupted. "She didn't even see you."

The door opened again. This time it was Jenny.

"Hey, you guys," she said. "How about holding it down! If someone comes by and hears this noise, we'll get a demerit."

"It's too late. We've already got ten of them," Judy said.

"Ten! What do you mean?" Jenny asked.

Jada explained what had happened, and Jenny turned to Brittany. "Didn't you know that was against the rules?"

"No. Sean said it would be all right as long as he stayed across the path."

"After dark, boys aren't even allowed on this side of the camp."

"I'm sorry. It won't happen again," Brittany said.

"I hope not. I'd like to win the Best Cabin contest this year, but we can't survive many setbacks like this."

When the room was quiet again, Jada asked, "Who wants to hear the end of the story I was telling?"

"I don't," Beth said. "I didn't like it."

"What story are you talking about?" Jenny asked.

"Jada was telling a ghost story," Rebecca said. "It was about a couple whose car runs out of gas, and the man leaves his wife and goes to see if he can find help—"

"Oh, that one," Jenny interrupted. "Don't worry about it, Beth. That story has been around for years. I heard it the first year I came to camp."

"My mother said she had heard it when she was at camp," Jada said.

Brittany crawled into bed and then realized that she had never gotten around to inflating her air mattress. It was going to be impossible to sleep with the springs poking through the cot and her sleeping bag, but she didn't want to take a chance on getting up and disturbing everyone else. They were angry enough at her as it was.

Long after the sound of deep, easy breathing filled the cabin, Brittany was still staring silently at the ceiling. She had never gone to sleep without reading or at least watching a few minutes of television, and the uncomfortable bed, the strange night noises and the presence of other people in the room were making it impossible to sleep.

A sound caught her ear, and she sat up in bed, straining to hear better. "Who is it?" she called out softly.

"It's me, Beth."

"What's wrong?"

"I can't sleep."

Brittany was already making her way across the room to Beth's bunk. "Why? Are you sick?"

"N-no," Beth's voice trembled. "I'm scared. That story..."

Brittany sat down on the edge of the bed and rubbed Beth's forehead. "It's all right. I know just how you feel," she said. "Do you want me to sit with you until you go back to sleep?"

"Would you mind?"

"No. In fact, I couldn't get to sleep myself."

She curled up on the foot of Beth's bed, and Beth stretched out, letting her feet rest against Brittany's knees. There was something relaxing about concentrating on the child's even breathing and slowly Brittany began to relax, only to be jolted back to attention by a sharp kick.

"Brittany?"

"Yes?"

"Just seeing if you were still awake," Beth murmured, turning over to her other side.

Twice more, before she finally slipped into a deep sleep, Beth checked to see that Brittany was still awake. Although she did doze off a couple of times, the sky was turning a pale gray before Brittany finally stretched out on her own bed.

Almost immediately, she started having a strange dream about people rushing around. There was a lot of noise and confusion, but she couldn't get away from it. She even thought she heard someone calling her.

Slowly she opened her eyes and saw Jenny leaning over her, shaking her.

"What are you doing still in bed?" Jenny asked. "I called you before I went to the bathroom."

Brittany was having a hard time keeping her eyes open, and she mumbled, "Wha...I can't...?"

"We have to be at the bleachers for the opening ceremony and raising of the flag in *eight* minutes."

"Eight minutes!" Brittany cried, swinging her feet to the floor and struggling to stand up. "I can't shower and get dressed in eight minutes."

Jenny was already on her knees, pulling suitcases out from under Brittany's bed. "Forget the shower, just get into some clothes," she said, pulling things out of Brittany's bags.

Brittany pushed her away. "Look," she said. "Why don't you and the girls go on ahead. I'll join you as soon as I'm dressed."

"That won't help. We all have to be there before the whistle."

The morning was a little chilly, so Brittany took out a pair of jeans, but she had to go to another suitcase to find a suitable top. She had just started brushing her hair when they heard the whistle.

The girls groaned, and Jenny said, "You can relax now. We just got five more demerits. I'll go ahead and take the girls to the flagpole so that they won't miss the entire ceremony. Catch up with us as soon as you can."

Brittany pulled her hair into twin ponytails and trimmed them with red ribbons that matched the appliqués on her shirt and her red sneakers. Finally, she added a touch of lipstick and then hurried to catch up with her cabin just as they were being dismissed for breakfast.

Compared to the other meals they'd shared, breakfast was unusually quiet, and Brittany knew it was all her fault. Fifteen demerits in less than twenty-four hours must be something of a record.

As soon as they finished eating, everyone separated to go to their own individual classes, and Brittany was glad to escape to the comparative privacy of the infirmary.

"Rough morning?" Betty asked as soon as she saw her.

Brittany nodded. "I'm afraid I'm not getting off to a very good start," she said.

"Don't let it get you down. Everyone has bad days," Betty said kindly.

She handed Brittany the key to the medicine cabinet and said, "I've already given Stephen Wheeler his allergy medicine, but Joshua Pocus and Traci Groot haven't come by yet. Miriam Clark is out with the list now, rounding up everyone who's supposed to take any kind of medicine or vitamins. Whenever they come in, be sure to double-check the name and dosage and then write it down."

"I will," Brittany said.

"I'm going to the cafeteria for breakfast, and then I'll be up front in my apartment if you need me," Betty said.

Left alone for the moment, Brittany looked around, familiarizing herself with the small office, the contents of the medicine cabinet and the location of the first-aid supplies. She was frequently interrupted by someone needing medication or a Band-Aid, but performing the simple tasks, even logging them on the medical chart, restored some of her self-confidence.

She had brought the camp handbook with her and when she wasn't busy, she studied it. She might get some more demerits, but it wasn't going to be because she didn't know the rules. When Betty came back to relieve her, she could recite most of them by heart.

"Do you need me for anything else?" she asked as she returned the keys.

"That's all right. The lunch whistle will go off in a few minutes, so you can go on back to your cabin."

Brittany started across the main compound but slowed up when she saw Sean coming toward her. "Where are you headed?" she asked.

"To the cafeteria. My cabin has to help serve today. Didn't you see me at breakfast this morning?"

Brittany shook her head. "I guess I wasn't paying attention."

"I thought you were angry with me for getting you into trouble last night. I really didn't know I wasn't supposed to be over there."

"It was just as much my fault." She held up the handbook. "But it's not going to happen to me again."

"Is there anything in there against taking a walk with me tonight?"

"No, but..."

"No *buts*. This is our night off, so I'll see you right after the campfire."

"Sean, I never said..." she began, but Sean was already running toward the cafeteria. Shaking her head, she turned around and almost bumped into George Howland.

"Is Sean giving you trouble?" he asked.

"No, of course not. He's very nice, but..."

"But you don't like nice guys?"

"Of course not! No, I don't mean that—I do like nice guys but that's not the problem. Oh, stop it!" She laughed. "What are you doing over here, anyway?"

"I'm on my way to the infirmary."

"What happened?"

"Nothing serious," he said, shrugging. "I got a scratch and figured I'd come over and let you kiss it and make it better."

"I think some antiseptic will probably do more for it," she said.

Suddenly the noon whistle blew, and Brittany gasped. "I've got to go!"

She started to run, but George caught her arm. "Can I see you later?"

"George, I have to go! If I cause my cabin to get another demerit..."

"What about tonight?" He was still holding tightly to her arm.

"Yes! Just let me go," she said, pulling away and running for her cabin.

She made it just in time, and without stopping to catch her breath, she fell into step at the end of the line.

The girls were more talkative than they had been that morning, but they continued to ignore Brittany. They were more interested in the relay races that would be held that afternoon. They were trying to figure out who, in their group, had any special athletic abilities.

After studying the handbook, Brittany knew that they could earn extra points by winning any of the competitions set up on the game field. She wished there was something she could do to help, but athletically speaking, she was hopeless. Besides, no one expected anything from her.

It was her turn to stay with the girls during the rest period, but Jenny followed them back to the cabin and waited until they were all settled in.

"You don't have to stay in your bunk or take a nap. Just keep the noise down to a dull roar until you hear the whistle," she said.

"Yeah, we've already lost enough points today," Nettie said.

"I can't stand any more of this!" Beth suddenly cried.

Jenny stopped at the door and looked back at Beth. "What do you mean?" she asked.

"It's my fault that Brittany overslept this morning."

"Beth, it's all right," Brittany said. "Don't—"

"It's not all right! Everyone is blaming you, but they should really be mad at me."

With her clenched hands Beth faced them defiantly. "After hearing that story last night, I couldn't get to sleep, so I asked Brittany to sit with me. She stayed on my bed all night."

Everyone was silent, looking from Beth to Brittany until Jenny asked, "Why didn't you tell me?"

Brittany shrugged. "I didn't think it was that important."

"Well, it is," Jenny said. "And I'm really sorry. I was so busy worrying about losing the Best Cabin contest that I didn't focus."

"I'm sorry, too," Nettie said.

"Me too!" "So am I." "I'm sorry," the rest of them added in a mixed chorus of apologies.

"Thanks, I appreciate this but I have to be honest with you. Even if I hadn't stayed up all night, I might have overslept, anyway. I've never gotten up early."

"Don't worry, we won't let you oversleep again," the girls assured her.

"Since you have things under control in here, I'm going to take my break," Jenny said. "When you hear the next whistle, bring the girls out to the playing field."

She started out the door and then ducked back inside. "I almost forgot. Don't plan anything for after the relay races. Our chore for the day is to police the area for any trash or broken equipment, and report anything that needs to be taken care of. Things like that.''

"That'll give us the perfect chance to start looking for things for the scavenger hunt," Jada said. "We can study the list now so that we'll know what to look for."

After Jenny left, they all gathered around Brittany's bed to look at the list. Before long there were shouts of "Hey, I have that! I brought one of those!"

Just going through their luggage, they managed to collect quite an impressive pile of things. There were pins, pink socks, a long piece of string, licorice candy and even some of the more unusual things such as a pocket knife, a classic novel and a can of shaving cream.

"What were you doing with shaving cream?" Pam asked when Melba brought it out.

"Well, at the camp I went to last summer, we put it all over our counselor's pillow—not that I'd do anything like that here," she added hastily.

"Remind me to check my pillow every night," Brittany said.

"Now that we have all this loot, where can we hide it?" Rebecca asked. "We don't want it getting misplaced or used for something else."

"What about one of my suitcases?" Brittany suggested. She pulled them out from under her bed and began rearranging things until she'd emptied one.

When the whistle blew again, it was time to assemble on the playing field for the relay races. There were a few of the usual type of races that included running, hopping and jumping, but most of the races were unusual—running while carrying an egg in a teaspoon or a balloon between your knees, or even building the highest human pyramid.

Fortunately for Brittany, athletic ability wasn't as important as the desire to win, and no one from her cabin was happier than she was that they managed to win two of the ten races.

Chapter Six

Instead of celebrating their small victory, Brittany and Jenny separated the girls into two groups and made a careful search of the campgrounds, turning up little litter and damaged camp equipment but finding eight more things for the scavenger hunt.

Afterward, while everyone else headed for the swimming pool or the lake, Brittany went to the showers. She hadn't had a chance to wash her hair since she'd arrived, and in another day it would be hanging around her face in limp strings.

She would have liked to spend some extra time after her shower on her clothes and makeup, but the handbook had said that dinner would be served at seven o'clock, and she knew that meant seven, not seven-fifteen.

The rigid time schedule and the omnipresent whistle made her appreciate her night off even more. After the closing ceremony around the campfire ended and Jenny had taken the girls back to their cabin, Brittany breathed a long sigh of relief.

It wasn't that she didn't like the younger girls or found it a chore to be with them, but this was her first real break since she had come to camp. The next few precious hours were hers to do with as she pleased.

She moved up closer to where the other junior counselors were grouped around the fire and saw Dave at the center of the group.

"What are you doing here?" she asked.

He was on his knees, brushing bits of wood and straw away from the fire, but he turned his head enough to smile up at her. "I work here, remember?"

"I know that, but I thought this was supposed to be Troy's night off?"

"Why?" he asked. His eyes darkened. "Did you need to see him about something?"

"I just..."

Glenda pushed herself into the circle around the fire and effectively blocked Brittany's view of Dave. "I didn't know you traded off nights with Troy so that you could tend to the fire," she said teasingly.

"I'm almost through," he said. "I just wanted to make sure that the fire didn't go anywhere."

"What that fire really needs is some marshmallows," George said.

George reached over and touched Brittany's arm. "Do you want to go over to the general store and get some?"

"If she does, it will be with me," Sean said, easing closer to Brittany's other side.

"What makes you say that?" George asked.

"I asked her earlier today."

"So did I," George said.

"Sean . . . George," Brittany said, reaching out to both of them. "Don't do this. It's all my fault. I know I said I would see you tonight, but that was before—I mean, something's come up."

"What are you talking about?" Sean asked.

"I'm sorry, I can't . . ." she began, desperately trying to think of something that would be acceptable to both boys. She looked around wildly and her eyes landed on Dave.

Suddenly, she knew what to do. "It's something I really need to talk to my cousin about, but since he's not here, I guess Dave will have to substitute for him."

"Why does it have to be him?" Sean asked.

"Because I promised her father I'd look out for her," Dave said.

"Maybe you should go get Troy for her," Glenda suggested.

"No, it's not an emergency," Brittany said, and then pulled George and Sean into her glance, "unless I can't get you two to forgive me. I'm really sorry."

"Hey! If you're willing to give up toasted marshmallows, it's your loss," George said, his humor restored.

"Another time." She smiled. "Okay?"

Not to be outdone, Sean said, "I'll take a rain check, too."

Brittany felt the tension ease and let out a sigh of relief.

"I have to stay here until the fire's out," Dave explained, "and then we can take a walk, and you can tell me what's bothering you."

"I'll watch the fire for you," Sandy said. "I want to see if George is going to come back with those marshmallows, anyway."

"Thanks, Sandy," Dave said, standing up and reaching for Brittany's hand.

They started toward the lake, but instead of going to the pier, Dave kept to the shadows on a path that led beneath the trees along the shore. The darkness gave him a good excuse to continue holding her hand, and he had no intention of giving it up one minute earlier than he had to.

"What's this?" he asked as his thumb felt its way around a ring with a large, rough setting.

Brittany felt the tug at her ring and glanced down to be sure of which one she was wearing. "A gift from Uncle Ed."

Dave drew her hand closer. "I've never seen one like this before. Is it expensive?"

Brittany shrugged. "I don't know. Uncle Ed had it made for me out of a gold nugget that he found. Why?"

"You probably shouldn't wear it out here," he said, finally releasing her hand as they stopped beside the lake. "If you lost it, you'd never be able to find it again."

"I suppose you're right. I'll put it in my suitcase when I get back to the cabin. I've already given up makeup. I might as well give up jewelry." She paused. "If I stay here any longer I'm going to start looking..."

She stopped, but Dave supplied the rest of the words. "Like the rest of us."

"I don't mean to be rude, but this really isn't the place for me. I like the people, especially Jenny, but I'd rather spend my time dressing up and wearing makeup than...going fishing."

"Is that what you wanted to see Troy about? You're ready to call it quits and go home?"

"No. I may not be cut out for roughing it, but I can last a week."

"Then why did you want to see Troy?"

"I didn't. In fact, I was glad that you were there instead. Troy would have never let me..."

"Use him?" Dave finished for her.

"I didn't mean that. I just needed a way to get out of there without making things worse with Sean or George."

"What were you thinking of when you made a date with both of them? Seeing them in shifts?"

"Of course not. It wasn't even my fault. I was—"

"I've heard that before," Dave interrupted. "There was the Sweetheart Banquet in junior high school, the Key Club dance last year..."

"But I never planned those things. They just happened."

And would continue to happen, Dave thought. Boys chasing Brittany was as normal and natural as the changing of the seasons. There would always be someone.

"Brittany..." he began, but Brittany heard the amusement in his voice.

Impulsively, she wrapped an arm around his middle and laid her head on his chest. "I'm so glad that you're here. I can always count on you."

Dave let his arm circle her shoulders, and for a brief moment he held her close.

"So tell me," she said. "Who do you like better, Sean or George?"

Abruptly, he pushed her away. "If you're asking me which one I'd rather date, the answer is neither."

"I meant for me, silly."

"Come on. I'd better get you back to your cabin," he said, brusquely.

"But it's only a few minutes after nine. Can't we stay out later?"

"Yeah, but I don't want to take a chance on you oversleeping again."

Without another word, he took her back to the path that led to her cabin and stood there until she turned the corner. Then, retracing his steps, he made his way back to his own cabin, carefully avoiding the group still gathered around the campfire.

"You're back early," Troy commented as Dave closed the cabin door behind him.

"Shut up," Dave growled.

"She shot you down again, did she? Some people just never learn."

The next morning, Troy led his group directly toward the girls from cabin four.

"I see you made it up on time this morning," Troy needled his cousin.

"Are you kidding? The girls got me out of bed and sent me off to the showers, and then they went back to sleep. I came back to the cabin and had to wake everyone else up." Brittany laughed.

"Serves you right."

"Maybe," she said without rancor, "but at least I got a picture of the sunrise over the lake. That's one of the items on the scavenger hunt, remember?"

"Oh, yeah," Troy said, finally looking at Jenny. "How are you doing with the scavenger hunt?"

"Pretty well, I think. We had a lot of the things in our luggage."

"I'm not surprised. Brittany brought everything she owned with her," Troy said.

"You're just jealous that you didn't think to bring more." Brittany laughed. She was determined that even her sour cousin wasn't going to spoil her mood this morning.

She got in line for breakfast and noticed Sandy Cross behind the buffet table, bringing out extra bowls for cereal. "Why do I think that it's not going to be too long before Jenny and I are back there?" Brittany asked.

"You got it," Sandy grinned.

Jenny winked at Sandy and said, "Wait'll she finds out what we have to do today."

"What's that?" Brittany asked.

"Oh, we get to clean the girls' bathroom this afternoon, that's all."

"How . . . wonderful," Brittany said. "What if we just forgot to do it?"

"And get twenty demerits? No thanks," Jenny said.

After they sat down at their table, Beth asked, "Brittany, are you going to come and watch my swimming lesson today?"

"I don't know. It depends on what time I get away from the infirmary."

"Have all of you signed up some class this morning?" Jenny asked. "If you haven't, let me know so that I can get you into something before I have to report to the crafts room."

They all produced their class cards, showing that they were going to be busy with a variety of things. The only dissension was that Marlene and Jada hadn't been able to get archery at the same time.

"That's all right," Jenny reassured them. "It'll give you a chance to meet some other people. Besides you'll be back together at lunch, and you can spend all afternoon together."

"You go ahead and get the girls settled," Brittany told Jenny when they finished breakfast. "I'll clean up the table."

"Thanks. If you run out of sick people and have some free time, come on over to the crafts hut, and I'll let you help make baskets," Jenny said as she herded the kids out.

Brittany cleaned off the table and made her way over to the infirmary. She pulled the door open and greeted Betty with a smile. "Everything okay?"

"So far, so good," Betty answered. "You certainly look better today."

"I feel much better," Brittany admitted.

Betty handed her the key to the medicine cabinet and picked up her beeper off the desk. She started to leave but saw Billy LeMoyne coming up the steps and held the door open for him.

"Good morning. Did you come by for your vitamins?" she asked.

"I don't know why I have to take them," he grumbled. "This is supposed to be a vacation."

Brittany unlocked the cabinet, took out Billy's vitamins and double-checked them against the master list. "Yes, it's really awful of your mother to be so concerned about your health, isn't it?" she said as she handed him a vitamin.

Billy took the vitamin without further complaints, and Brittany noted it on the chart.

"Since you have this under control, I'll be on my way," Betty said. "I'll be in the cafeteria if you need me."

For the next hour, Brittany stayed busy, and then, as she'd been the day before she was suddenly alone. She already knew the camp handbook by heart, so she picked up a first-aid manual that was lying on the desk.

She hadn't even finished reading the first chapter when she heard someone coming. Looking up, she saw Dave walking up the steps with a crying child in his arms.

"What happened?" she asked, hurrying over to open the door for him.

"He tripped and scratched himself up," Dave said, putting the little boy down on the examination table. "His name is Ronnie Downs."

Brittany could see that Ronnie was trying to control his sobs, but the effort was causing his whole body to jerk. There were several angry scratches on his legs and one knee was badly skinned, but as soon as she knew that his injuries weren't life threatening, she relaxed.

"Where does it hurt?" she gently asked him.

"M-my arm," he said.

"You scratched your leg," Dave pointed out, but Brittany was already looking at the hand, which was red and puffy near the wrist.

"Did you fall on your hand or put it out to catch yourself?" she asked.

"I don't remember."

She left him long enough to put in a call to Betty and then took a cold pack from the refrigerator and put it on Ronnie's wrist. She gathered up the antiseptics and cloths for cleaning and bandaging the wounds and put them on the table beside him.

Ronnie started to move his leg out of her reach, but Brittany persisted. "Just let me look at it," she said.

The scratches weren't very deep, but there was a lot of dirt and debris in them. "I think you're going to live," she said lightly, "but we're going to have to clean up these scratches."

"Will it hurt?" Ronnie asked.

"You'll feel it, but it won't hurt any more than it does now. And as soon as it's clean, it can start getting well," she said. "I'm glad you're such a big boy. If you were crying and jerking around, it would hurt worse."

"It hurts now," he said.

"I know." She began cleaning one of the scratches.

Betty came through the door on a run. "What is it?"

"Ronnie fell down. I don't think these scratches are that serious, but I think you should see his wrist," Brittany said.

Betty removed the cold pack and felt Ronnie's wrist. "I don't think it's broken, but I'm going to take him to the hospital for X rays just to be sure."

Betty went to the files to get Ronnie's medical release form. "Finish cleaning up the scratches but don't bandage them. The hospital will want to see them too," she said.

As soon as she was through, Brittany took a pillow from one of the sickbeds. "Do you want to use this to cushion his wrist on the way to the hospital?" she asked.

"Yes, thanks," Betty said, tucking the pillow under her arm. "Mrs. Clark is at the swimming pool. I'll go by and tell her to listen for you, but you'll have to stay here until I get back."

"That's all right," Brittany said.

"Do you want me to carry Ronnie to the car for you?" Dave asked.

"I can walk," Ronnie said.

Betty hesitated and then shrugged. "I think we'll be all right."

After they'd left, Brittany reached for the chart to list the injury. Dave hadn't moved, so she asked, "Was there anything else?"

He shook his head and sat down on the corner of her desk. "You're pretty good at this," he said.

"That was my first real injury. Up to now, I've only handed out vitamins and allergy pills. I do like it, though. I've even started thinking about becoming a doctor."

"Dave?" Glenda called, staring at them through the screen door. "Are you coming back to finish the boating lesson?"

"I guess so," Dave said, standing up and pushing away from the desk. "I was just getting Ronnie taken care of."

"Oh? Where is he?" Glenda asked.

"Betty took him in to be X-rayed," Brittany answered.

Glenda looked back at Dave. "Then you're through here, right?" she asked, holding the door open for him.

"I guess so," he said, following her.

Watching them leave for the lake, Brittany was surprised by a catch in her throat. Jenny had hinted that there had been something going on between Dave and Glenda last summer. Perhaps there still was.

Chapter Seven

The lunch whistle had already blown before Betty and Ronnie, his wrist wrapped in an elastic bandage, returned to camp, and Mrs. Clark came to relieve Brittany from the infirmary.

She went directly to the cafeteria, but Jenny and the girls were almost through eating.

"Sorry I'm late," Brittany said, as she joined them. "I hope that didn't cause us to get any more demerits."

"No, everyone knew where you were," Jenny said. "By the way, how is the little boy?"

"He's going to be fine. The doctor said it was just a sprain."

"Brittany," Beth interrupted, "can you come out to the pool this afternoon so that I can show you a new dive that I learned?"

"I guess so."

"Don't forget that we have to clean the bathrooms," Jenny reminded them.

"Does anyone know what we're going to play after rest period?" Marlene asked.

"On my way over here I saw them putting up some volleyball nets," Melba said.

"Maybe I should clean the bathroom while the rest of you are playing," Brittany said.

"Oh, you can play volleyball," Jada said. "It's not very hard."

Jada sounded so serious that Brittany couldn't help laughing. "Thanks for your concern. I'm sorry to be so much of a burden."

"You're not a burden," Beth said. "We know you're doing the best that you can."

That made everyone laugh. As soon as the laughter died, Jenny began hurrying them along. "Come on, you guys. Finish eating so we can get back to the cabin. I want all of you to write your parents today. We get a bonus point if everyone writes at least one letter home."

"You're really determined to win that Best Cabin thing, aren't you?" Nettie said.

Jenny stopped abruptly. "I'm doing it again, aren't I?" she said. "If the rest of you don't really care about winning, you're just going to have to keep reminding me."

"No, we want to win," Jada said.

"Do you really think we can?" Brittany asked. "I've cost us so many points."

"Even if we don't win, if we could come in second or third, we'd have some choice about what we'd have to do for the banquet. I don't want to get stuck having to clean up afterward," Jada said.

"Or entertain. That would be even worse!" Marlene said.

Still discussing their chances of winning, the girls let Jenny nudge them back to their cabin, while Brittany, free for the next hour, headed for the pier. It wasn't the assigned meeting place, but everyone just naturally gravitated toward it. Today, Sean was waiting for her with a canoe.

"Come on," he called. "I got permission to take you for a ride."

After being shut up in the infirmary all morning, Brittany would have preferred taking a walk or even going for a swim, but she didn't want to hurt his feelings.

"Okay, thanks," she said.

Dave was sitting on the pier showing George and Sandy how to string a fishing pole while Glenda sunned herself nearby. As Brittany and Sean walked past, he said, "Don't forget to take some life preservers."

"Why? I can swim, and the water's not swift or dangerous," Sean said.

"Sorry. Those are the rules," Dave said.

Sean didn't move toward the life preservers, so Dave got up and took one from the stack beside the boat-house and handed it to Brittany. Obediently, she slipped the orange apparatus over her head and tried to reach the strings, but she couldn't see over its bulk.

Dave tied them for her and then gave a tug to make sure the life preserver was secure. "Keep it on," he said.

Sean put on a life preserver, but he grumbled as he put the canoe into the water, "Maybe you should get a canoe and follow us."

"Maybe I will."

Brittany moved between them quickly but as she stepped into the boat, it gave a crazy lurch, and she grabbed for Dave.

"Are you going to be all right?" he asked, settling her onto a seat.

"She'll be fine," Sean said, climbing aboard and pushing away from shore. He gave several powerful strokes, and the light canoe glided quickly toward the center of the lake.

As soon as they were out far enough, Sean pulled off his life preserver and dropped it to the bottom of the canoe. "He can make me take it, but I don't have to keep it on," he said. "Do you want to take yours off?"

"No, I'm fine," Brittany said.

"What's the matter? Don't you think I could save you?"

"It's not that. Besides, I know how to swim, too, but it's not that uncomfortable."

"Maybe not. I just don't like his attitude."

"What do you mean?"

"In case you hadn't noticed, he acts as though he owns you."

"I told you before—Dave is just a friend of the family."

Sean grinned and let his voice drop to a deeper note. "You can be sure that if I'd known you for a long time, we would be a lot more than just friends."

Brittany wasn't sure how to reply, so she didn't say anything. Sean was so handsome, but his heavy flattery and constant flirting made her uncomfortable. If only he had George's sense of humor.

In fact, she thought, a perfect guy would be a blend of those two—someone as good-looking as Sean but with George's personality. Someone like . . . Dave.

David. Why in the world had she thought of him? She leaned back and let her hands trail along in the water, watching the ripples as they rushed in widening circles to the shore.

A bit of bright purple caught her eye, and she turned to stare at it. It wasn't faded or torn, just a scarf or some kind of ribbon with one end tied to a low-hanging tree limb and the other end disappearing into the water. Even after they had passed, she continued to stare at it.

Puzzled by her preoccupation, Sean asked, "What's the matter?"

"Nothing." She shrugged. "It's so peaceful out here. I was just letting my mind wander."

"You certainly look contented."

"Do you want me to paddle for a while and let you rest?" she asked.

"No, you just enjoy the ride. I'm happy just watching you."

Again, Brittany smiled vaguely and then changed the subject to talk about him until it was time to head back to camp. Before they reached the shore, Brittany could see that the pier was already deserted.

"Sean, hurry or we're going to be late for the games!" she urged.

"We won't be that late. I haven't heard the whistle."

"Maybe we missed it," she said, hopping out before he could help her. "If I cause my cabin to get any more demerits, they'll kill me."

She tried to untie her life preserver, but she couldn't see what she was doing, and rather than waste time fighting it, she shucked the thing off over her head.

Sean was tying up the canoe, so she grabbed his preserver from the bottom of the canoe and took both of them back to their proper stacks. They started for the field together, but she couldn't stand the slow pace that Sean set and ran on ahead. She was completely out of breath when she finally joined Jenny.

"Are you all right?" Jenny asked.

"That depends," she puffed. "Did I make it in time?"

Jenny nodded. "Some of the cabins are still choosing sides. We're going to be paired with Troy and Dave's cabin. Is that all right?"

"How did that happen?" Brittany asked.

"Troy asked me if we would be on their team," Jenny said.

"Are you sure that he remembers I'm in your cabin?"

"Of course. Why do you ask?"

"If my cousin wants you to be his partner even though he knows it will mean getting me in the bargain, he must really like you," Brittany said.

Jenny blushed, but before she could say anything, the boys joined them. Troy went immediately to Jenny's side, and Dave spoke to Brittany.

"I see you made it back from your canoe ride," he said.

"Just in the nick of time. I seem to be living on the edge this week, either getting demerits or just missing them. We could really use the extra points for winning today."

Dave grinned. "How good are you at volleyball?"

"About the same as any other sport—terrible," she said. "But I promise to try and stay out of everyone's way."

Coach gave all the teams five minutes to get ready for the first game, and Jenny, Troy and Dave went to work immediately, lining up the players so that a strong player was behind each weak one. Brittany kept her mouth shut and let them move her around as they were doing with the smaller kids. She felt better when Dave took up a spot behind her.

Once the games had started, there was little time to think about anything else. Sometimes the ball flew past Brittany so fast that she didn't even have time to duck. She even caught on to how to set it up so that Dave could spike it back over the net.

There wasn't time for anyone to show off his skill or finesse, but it didn't really matter. Brittany enjoyed the camaraderie of her team and noted with pride that Troy didn't shout at her or put her down once during the entire afternoon. All in all, their team played in eight games, and since they only lost one, they were the overall champions.

"I have a great idea how we can celebrate," Jenny said. "Everyone grab a sponge and some disinfectant, and we'll go clean the bathroom."

"That's *celebrating*?" Brittany laughed.

"Well, it's got to be done, and the sooner we finish, the sooner we can all go swimming!"

They knew that she was right, and besides, they were so excited about winning that they were still laughing when they opened the bathroom door. Then all laughter stopped.

The bathroom was a total disaster. The floor was covered with gooey, wet toilet tissue, the mirrors and walls were smeared with toothpaste, and petroleum jelly was on all of the fixtures.

"Holy moly," Pam said, breaking the silence. "What happened here?"

"Everyone was at the games. Who could have done this?" Judy asked.

"And why?" someone else asked.

Jenny and Brittany were walking around surveying the damage and shaking their heads.

"It's my guess that someone was unhappy that we won the volleyball games," Jenny said.

"But it isn't fair. It's going to take us hours to get this place cleaned up," Beth said.

"Not if we get busy," Jenny said. "Come on, start sweeping that stuff up off the floor. Marlene, you and Jada do the mirrors, and Brittany and I will do the toilets."

It took them longer than the allotted thirty minutes to get the bathroom back in order, and when they'd finally finished, Nettie said, "I don't know about the rest of you, but now I really want to win that Best Cabin contest. Let's show whoever did this to us that we can win in spite of them."

"That'd serve them right," Beth said.

"How can we tell where we stand now?" Judy asked.

"They keep a running tally of each cabin's points on a big scoreboard near the flagpole. We'll check it when we go to the campfire after dinner," Jenny said.

Brittany was as interested as the campers were to see exactly what it would take for them to win, and she was relieved to find out that the situation wasn't as hopeless as she'd thought. They were still in last place, but with the extra points they had earned in the volleyball game, they were only seven points behind the next-to-the-last cabin and seventeen points behind the first-place cabin.

"If we don't lose any more points, and somehow manage to win the scavenger hunt, we could pull it off," Jenny said.

"How many more items do we have to find?" Jada asked.

"I haven't counted them today, but we already had half of them yesterday," Brittany said.

"Yes, but if it was that easy for us, you can bet the other cabins won't have any trouble, either. We're going to have to turn our attention to the harder, more unusual things."

"I started a book of wildflowers. That's on the list," Rebecca said.

"That's exactly the thing I was talking about," Jenny said approvingly.

"Well, I don't know how good it is."

"Don't worry about that. Bring it with you to the crafts hut tomorrow, and I'll help you with it."

They were so busy planning their strategies that Brittany didn't know Sean was anywhere around until he asked, "Where were you after the volleyball game this afternoon?"

She made a wry face at him and said, "Cleaning the bathroom."

"That's one thing I don't like about this place," Sean said. "I don't see why we have to do janitor's work."

"For one thing, it helps to keep the cost of the camp down. If the Walkers had to hire other people to come in and clean and take care of some of the things that we do, either we counselors wouldn't get paid as much or the kids would have to pay twice as much to come," Jenny said.

Beverly Adams had walked up, and now she joined the conversation. "Besides, the chores aren't that bad," she remarked.

"Well, we had a slight complication, but it wasn't anything that we couldn't overcome," Jenny said.

While Jenny and Beverly were talking, Sean leaned closer to Brittany and whispered. "Can I see you after the campfire?"

She shook her head. "I won't have time tonight. We need the extra point for being the first cabin to get its lights off, so we're going to..."

"Don't tell me that you're getting all caught up in this contest thing."

"Sure, don't you want to win?"

"I'm more interested in spending time with you."

"But if we both won, then we could go to the banquet together," she said.

"You don't really believe that, do you?"

"Of course I do. Why not?"

"Can't you tell that the Walkers' nephew is going to win the boys' division."

"His cabin is ahead right now, but that doesn't mean he's going to win," Brittany said. "Look at us. We're in last place, and we're still trying."

"Yeah, but the Walkers don't have a niece. That means you still have a chance. Good old Dave probably helped them write up the rules for the contest."

"That's not true."

"How do you know?"

IT'S A JACKPOT OF A GREAT OFFER!

- 4 exciting First Love from Silhouette novels—FREE!
- a folding umbrella—FREE!
- a surprise mystery bonus that will delight you—FREE!

Silhouette Folding Umbrella— ABSOLUTELY FREE

You'll love your Silhouette umbrella. Its bright color will cheer you up on even the gloomiest day. It's made of rugged nylon to last for years, and is so compact (folds to 15″) you can carry it in your bag. This folding umbrella is yours free with this offer.

But wait . . . there's even more!

Free Home Delivery!

Subscribe to First Love from Silhouette and enjoy the convenience of previewing new, hot-off-the-press books every month, delivered right to your home. Each book is yours for only $1.95. And there's no extra charge for postage and handling!

Special Extras—Free!

You'll also get our free monthly newsletter—the indispensable insider's look at our most popular writers and their upcoming novels. Now you can have a behind-the-scenes look at the fascinating world of First Love. It's an added bonus you'll look forward to every month. You'll also get additional free gifts from time to time as a token of our appreciation for being a home subscriber.

DETACH AND MAIL CARD TODAY

PLAYER'S SCORECARD

MAIL TODAY

4 FREE BOOKS

FREE FOLDING UMBRELLA

Did you win a
mystery gift?

Place sticker here

Yes! I hit the jackpot. I have affixed my 3 hearts. Please send my 4
First Love from Silhouette novels free, plus my free folding umbrella
and free mystery gift. Then send me 4 books every month as they
come off the press, and bill me just $1.95 per book, with no extra
charges for postage and handling.

If I am not completely satisfied, I may return a shipment and cancel
at any time. The free books, folding umbrella and mystery gift
remain mine to keep.   CJF037

NAME _____

ADDRESS _____

APT. _____

CITY _____

STATE _____

ZIP CODE _____

SILHOUETTE "NO-RISK" GUARANTEE
• There is no obligation to buy—the free books and gifts remain yours to keep.
• You receive books before they're available in stores.
• You may end your subscription anytime—just let us know.
Terms and prices subject to change. Offer limited to one
per household and not valid for
present subscribers.

PRINTED IN U.S.A.

Mail this card today for
4 FREE BOOKS
this folding umbrella and
a mystery gift ALL FREE!

"For one thing, my cousin is Dave's cabin mate. Do you think he's in on it, too?" she asked sharply.

"I forgot about Troy, but . . ."

Coach had moved to the front of the flagpole, and as he lit the bonfire, Brittany stalked off to take her place beside Jenny.

How dare Sean accuse the Walkers of cheating! Such a thing wasn't even worth discussing with Jenny. Besides, she knew that her friend was hoping Troy's cabin would win. If both their cabins won, Jenny would be paired with Troy, and she would be with Dave. Somehow, it was an intriguing idea.

She was so caught up in her own thoughts that she didn't hear very much of the lecture about the Indians that had once lived in the region. Afterward, the only thing she could remember was that the Indians had believed that earthquakes were caused by the steps of a gigantic, slow-moving turtle.

Chapter Eight

The scavenger hunt seemed to be on everyone's mind the next day. The whole camp was scrambling around trying to find things they might have overlooked before.

Since Brittany had to be on duty at the infirmary, she used her time to study the list of items and reported back to her cabin at lunch. "I think we're doing pretty well. We already have thirty-four of the fifty things," she said.

"Yes, but we don't know what the other cabins have," Jenny said.

"Dave came by the infirmary, and he said that he and Troy only had twenty-six."

"And we still have the rest of today and tomorrow," Marlene said.

"Some of the things are pretty strange, but we should be able to find a bird's nest or an arrowhead, and what about a seashell? Has anyone looked for one over by the pier?" Brittany asked.

"Brittany, that body of water out there is a lake, not an ocean," Judy said.

"I know that, but if they have shells on the list, then they must have scattered some around somewhere."

"I have a paper target from a bull's-eye that was scored in archery this morning," Melba said.

"You hit a bull's-eye?" Marlene asked.

"I didn't. One of the boys in class hit two, so I asked him if I could have one of them."

"Good for you. There's nothing in the rules that say we have to score a bull's-eye. Just get one without stealing or buying," Jenny said.

"Did you put it in my suitcase?" Brittany asked. "I left it unlocked so any of you could get to it."

"It's all taken care of," Melba said.

"After lunch, Troy and I are going to hike back into the woods and look for the treasure chest," Jenny said. "The list says it's a buried treasure, but we can't dig it out of the ground, so it must be in one of the caves or gullies up in the hills."

"What are you going to do if you find it? I mean, who gets to keep it?" Nettie asked.

"We've already discussed that," Jenny said. "The first person who spots it, gets it. It's the only fair way."

"Well, try to keep him distracted so that he doesn't look too closely," Brittany said.

"That's more along your line," Jenny grinned as she got up to take her tray away.

Brittany and the rest of the girls followed suit, but while Jenny went off to meet Troy, they headed back to the cabin.

After everyone had settled down with a game or a book, Brittany got out her mirror and combs. She had heard they were going to play capture-the-flag that afternoon, and if she was going to do all that running, she had to do something with her hair. A single braid would probably work best, she thought.

Since she was going to change into a pink-and-lavender jump suit before going back out, she decided to weave ribbons of pink, lavender and a deeper purple into the braid. She laid the ribbons on the foot of her bed and started to climb on it and get settled when they skittered to the floor.

She bent over to pick them up, and when she did, the sight of the ribbons dangling from her hand struck a sensitive chord. In her mind's eye, there was a clear image of another purple ribbon hanging... in a tree. What on earth was a ribbon doing in a tree?

It couldn't have gotten there unless someone put it there, and no one except the Walkers had access to that particular portion of the lake. What possible motive could they have for doing such a thing, unless it had something to do with the scavenger hunt!

There was nothing on the scavenger list about a purple scarf or ribbon, but maybe it was something else. Maybe it was marking the spot where something else was hidden. The treasure chest? Could it be buried in water?

She was so excited that she couldn't do her hair and ended up gathering it into a simple ponytail. Then she changed clothes and paced the floor until Jenny returned, empty-handed.

"Nothing, huh?" she asked.

"Not a thing," Jenny said. "I don't know where that treasure chest could be unless someone has already found it and they're just not telling."

Just then, the whistle blew, and Brittany motioned for the girls to head on out to the recreation field while she hung back with Jenny.

"I saw something strange out on the lake yesterday," she said. "I think it might be a clue or something, so I'm going back to check it out as soon as the games are over."

"I'll go with you," Jenny said.

"I don't know. People might get suspicious if we leave together."

"But you can't go alone. You don't even know how to handle a canoe."

Brittany had already thought of that. "I'll ask Dave to take me," she said.

She didn't have to wait very long for an opportunity to talk to him. Minutes after the game began, Dave captured her not more than ten feet from her base.

"I'm glad it was you," she said while he was leading her away to a stockade inside his territory. "Can I ask you something?"

Dave grinned down at her. "This is war; I'm not making any deals."

"I'm not talking about this game. I need a favor."

"What is it?"

"Could you take me out in a canoe this afternoon?"

"Why me?"

"I'll explain everything later. Is it all right, though? I mean, will you take me?"

"Sure. No problem."

"Good." She smiled. "Now let's talk about an early parole."

Dave's confusion lasted for only a second. "I'm a soldier who's loyal to my team," he said, "but you might be able to sway me with the right offer."

"Such as?"

"Go on. I'll collect my payment later."

Brittany started running, but before she ever reached the safety of her own territory, she was captured again. This time it was by a girl from G2. She spent the rest of the game as a prisoner of war, watching her team lose its flag and eventually the contest.

When the game was finally called, it was judged a tie between the strong girls' team that Glenda captained and Dave's team.

"Darn," Jenny said afterward. "We really could have used another victory. That puts Glenda's cabin five more points out in front."

"We still have the scavenger hunt," Brittany reminded her. "Dave said he'd take me out to look for that scarf."

"I hope you find something. While you're gone, I'll keep an eye on the girls."

When Brittany reached the pier, Dave was already waiting for her. She slipped a life vest over her head and climbed into the canoe. "Come on, let's go," she said.

"What's the hurry?" he asked, going to her and checking the side ties. "Are you afraid Sean might catch you going off with me?"

"I don't care what Sean thinks. I just don't want anyone following us."

Dave pushed off, and when they were away from shore, he asked, "When are you going to tell me what this is all about?"

"I saw something out here yesterday, and I needed someone I could trust to bring me back to check it out."

"And that's why you asked me?"

"Of course. Who else?"

It wasn't exactly the motivation he wanted, but at least it was something. Aloud, he asked, "Which way?"

Brittany pointed to the right, and Dave turned the canoe in that direction, his powerful strokes moving them quickly through the water. They traveled in silence for a few minutes, and then, just when Brittany was about to believe the scarf had been a figment of her imagination, she saw it again.

"There it is!" she cried, pointing to the little scrap of cloth.

"What?"

"That scarf or whatever it is. Can you get me closer to it?"

Dave maneuvered her end of the canoe around until she could reach the bright, purple ribbon. One end of it was still tied securely to the tree limb, and when she pulled it, she felt resistance at the other end.

"There's something down there," she said, pulling faster on the ribbon. A moment later, a small metal box broke the surface of the water.

"Hey! Is that what I think it is?" Dave shouted.

Brittany was fumbling with the strings and latches. "I don't know. I can't get it open."

Dave pulled out a small pocketknife and took the box from her. After he cut the strings, he worked the top loose with the edge of the knife and held it out to her. "You want to do the honors?" he asked.

She started to reach for it and then changed her mind. "What if we're wrong? You'd better look first."

Afraid to look but too excited to hide her eyes, Brittany compromised by watching Dave's face and started smiling as soon as he did.

"It's the treasure chest, all right," he said, turning it around so that she could see the shiny golden chains, glass necklaces and rings and dime-store bracelets.

"Really! I can't believe it! I found it!"

She was having a hard time keeping still, and her erratic movements were causing the canoe to take some funny dips.

"Hey, careful, or you're going to dump us right in the middle of the lake!"

"I don't care! I want to jump and dance!"

"Fine. As soon as we get us to shore, you can hug me, but until then, you'd better put it on my account," he said as he started rowing back to camp.

"I feel as though I'd found a real treasure chest," she said, slipping the costume jewelry on her hands and arms. "What's everyone going to think when I come back decked out like this?"

"Maybe you should keep it hidden."

"Why?"

"Well, if no one knows you've already found it, they'll waste time looking for it and won't look for some of the other things that they could find."

"I guess there's nothing wrong with that," she said. "But how am I going to get it back to my cabin without anyone seeing me?"

"I'll let you off on the bank behind the girls' bathroom. All you'll have to do is go over the hill and sneak into your cabin."

"How do I know I can trust you to keep my secret?"

"I can be bribed." He eased the canoe to the bank and held it there until she got out. "How about meeting me after the campfire tonight, so I can collect what you owe me?"

"I guess I should. I can't afford to let it keep building up interest."

A noise from the top of the hill distracted them, and nervous about holding the chest out in full view of anyone who happened by, Brittany hurried up the hill to her cabin.

Once she was safely inside, she reopened the treasure chest and spread the contents out on her bed. She was so busy going through the trinkets that she didn't hear the door open.

"You found it!" Jenny gasped.

"Isn't it wonderful?" Brittany said, holding up a handful of fake jewels. After Jenny had a chance to let the significance of the chest sink in, Brittany told her about Dave's advice to keep it to themselves.

"That's a good idea," Jenny said. "Maybe we shouldn't even tell our girls."

"Why not? They're on our side."

"I know, but if they know we have the chest, they won't try as hard."

"You're probably right. Besides, they might let it slip that we've found it," Brittany said. "I'll put it in one of my other suitcases."

She pulled out another suitcase and made room in it for the little chest. "By the way," she asked, "how did you know I was back?"

"When I saw you and Dave row past the pier, I figured something was up, so I headed back here."

"Do you think anyone else noticed?"

"They noticed, all right, but don't worry. From the comments I heard, they just thought you two wanted a little more time together."

"But we're not—" Brittany started to protest but caught herself. "He asked me to meet him after the campfire tonight," she said.

"So there is something going on between you two!"

"Not exactly—not yet, anyway," Brittany replied with a grin. "At home, he and Troy would never let me hang around with them. Most of the time I didn't even think he liked me."

Jenny sat down on Brittany's cot and wrapped her arms around her legs and rested her chin on top of her knees. "Oh, sure," she said. "Every boy in camp, except for Troy, has been trying to get a date with you, and you think Dave isn't interested."

For a minute, Brittany was lost in her own thoughts, and then she asked, "Have you ever been in love?"

"Gosh, I don't know. I've had crushes on a lot of different boys, but I don't think any of them were the real thing. What about you?"

Brittany shook her head. "I've never even had a crush. Every time I thought I might like someone, we'd go out, and I don't know, he'd seem so ordinary."

"That's the difference in us," Jenny said. "I'd sit home and dream about dating certain boys, and you'd do it." She picked up a pillow and threw it at Brittany. "Come on. We'd better get ready for dinner."

Dave hadn't said where they should meet, so after dinner and the evening ceremony, Brittany wandered over to the campfire to wait for him. Sandy and George were already there, toasting marshmallows, and she joined them.

Soon, she heard footsteps behind her and was surprised to hear Glenda ask, "What are you doing here?"

"This is my off-duty night. Where should I be?"

Glenda shrugged. "I thought you were in your cabin. I just passed Jenny on the way to the infirmary."

"You don't think something's wrong, do you?" Sandy asked. "It's almost time for the last whistle. If someone's not in the cabin with your girls..."

"I'd better go check," Brittany said.

Some of the cabins, including her own, had already turned off their lights, and she knew she didn't have much time. She started running, and though she was gasping for breath, she managed to make it over the threshold just as the whistle blew.

Her eyes hadn't adjusted to the darkness, so she stopped at the door and called out, "Is...is everything all right?"

"Brittany? What are you doing here?" Jenny asked.

"I thought you were in the infirmary," Brittany said, making her way to her friend's bed.

"I walked over there with Rebecca to get a Band-Aid for her finger," Jenny said. "But Mrs. Clark was watching the cabin until I got back."

There was a soft knock on the door, and Betty poked her head inside. "Just making a bed check," she said. "Everyone accounted for?"

"Yes," Jenny answered, and Brittany added, "We're all fine."

"Oh, both of you are here. Then I'll mark you all as being safely inside for the night," she said, backing out.

As soon as she'd left, Brittany said, "Since you're here, I'll go back..."

Jenny caught her arm. "Brittany, you *can't* leave. Once you've been checked in you can't go back outside."

"But I have to! I'm supposed to meet Dave."

"You know the rules."

"Jenny, if I'm not out there, Dave's going to think I stood him up."

"You can explain it to him tomorrow."

"But that's not the same!" She flung herself on her bed. "Oh, I don't believe this!"

Chapter Nine

Brittany went to bed, but she had a hard time getting to sleep. Several times during the night, she found herself wide awake, staring at the ceiling without the slightest knowledge of what had wakened her.

Finally, just as dawn was beginning to break, she decided that she might as well get up.

Jenny heard her moving around and sat up in bed. "What's the matter?" she asked groggily.

Brittany waved her back down. "Go on back to sleep. I'm just going to take a shower and condition my hair. The ends are beginning to look awful."

"You're crazy," Jenny mumbled, snuggling deeper into her sleeping bag.

"No, I'm not. I'll be through before the rest of you get up."

She slipped her robe over her pajamas and gathered up everything she was going to need and headed for the bathroom. Although she would have preferred a private bathroom inside the cabin, she enjoyed the dewy freshness of the early morning walk, especially when she was the only one up and knew there would be plenty of hot water.

Taking her time, she shampooed her hair thoroughly and then, while she was waiting for the conditioner to work, she took a long, leisurely shower. She stayed under the water until her fingers and toes began to pucker, and then reluctantly she rinsed off and reached for the towel she'd left on the bench just outside.

She dried off, and with the towel wrapped around her, she stepped out of the shower to get the other towel for her wet hair.

It wasn't on the bench.

Curious, she stepped away from the shower, looked around and then walked back. She knew she had put the towel on the bench with her robe and clean clothes.

Then it hit her. It wasn't just the towel. Everything—her clothes, robe, hair dryer—everything was gone! All she had was the one towel.

For a brief moment, she considered trying to sneak back to her cabin, but she peeked outside and dismissed the idea. It was too big a risk. Instead, she paced the floor, going from the shower back to the door every few minutes. She had no idea what time it was when she began hearing people moving around outside.

Sometimes, in order to save a few minutes, the girls went to the bathroom *after* the flag ceremony. What if they did that today?

Just as she was about to panic and start screaming for help, the door opened and Beverly Adams walked in.

"Am I glad to see you!" Brittany gasped.

"Why? What's the matter?"

"Someone stole my clothes."

"You're kidding!"

"Well, I know I brought them with me, and they're not here now," Brittany said. "I hate to bother you, but could you please go by my cabin and tell Jenny what happened? I need her to bring me some more things."

"Of course. I'll go now," Beverly said without hesitation, and in just a few minutes, Jenny was back with her clothes.

"I found these behind our cabin," she said, handing them to Brittany.

"I suppose they walked back by themselves," Brittany muttered, checking to see if everything was there.

"You didn't hear anything?" Jenny questioned.

"No, but I was under the water."

"Who would do a thing like that, and why?"

Brittany was pulling on her clothes so fast that her voice shook, "Someone who wanted to make sure I wouldn't make it to the flagpole in time for the morning ceremony."

"Omigosh!" Jenny gasped. "I'd better go hurry our girls along. We'll meet you there if you...well, just do the best you can!"

"You go get the girls. I'll be there," Brittany promised.

Her hair was still soaking wet, but she didn't have time to do more than run a comb through it a couple of times. That and a touch of lipstick were all she bothered with.

Her cabin was already deserted, so she threw her things on her bed and raced to the flagpole, taking her position just seconds before the whistle blew.

As soon as the brief ceremony was over, Jenny caught her arm. "I can't believe you made it in time."

"Me either, but I'm going to have to skip breakfast so that I can finish dressing."

"You can't. We have to work in the cafeteria today, remember? We're supposed to be there right now."

"Oh, no," Brittany moaned. "I don't believe this day, and it's only seven o'clock in the morning!"

Jenny tried to console her. "At least you know it can only get better."

"I hope you're right," Brittany sighed. "Maybe everyone'll be too hungry to notice how I look."

Some of the campers were already lined up at the door, and as soon as Brittany and Jenny walked inside, Mrs. Jackson put them to work. Brittany was assigned to fill the juice glasses, and pretty soon she was too busy to worry about her appearance.

She wasn't even aware of who was going through the line until she heard Glenda remark slyly, "Why, Brittany, you're all wet."

Brittany glanced up, but when she saw that Dave, already several people away, had walked past her without speaking, she forgot all about her irritation with Glenda.

Darn! She'd missed him!

The only good thing about serving in the cafeteria was knowing that she would get to see Dave. She had to explain about last night, and the sooner, the better.

On an ordinary day, she could count on seeing him any number of times, but today, when it really mattered, she couldn't even find him. If it had been anyone else, she might have thought he was purposely avoiding her, but she couldn't believe it of Dave. It had to be just another strange coincidence.

After missing him again at lunch, she decided to stop waiting for him to come to her and began to actively search for him. Knowing that everyone on break eventually went down to the pier, she staked out a spot on the path and waited.

When she saw him coming, she stood up, but if he saw her, he gave no indication. She waited until he was almost on her and called out to him.

"Yeah?" he asked, finally coming to a stop.

Brittany sensed his impatience and asked quickly, "Can we talk?"

Dave's jaw tightened. "About what?"

"I wanted to explain about last night," she began awkwardly. "I told you that I'd meet you, but . . ."

"Oh, that." He shrugged. "Don't worry about it. I was just teasing you."

The blood drained away from her head so quickly that she felt light-headed. She had to force her lips to move. "That's what I thought," she said stiffly.

Afraid that her composure might slip, Brittany whirled around and went back to her cabin. If she could have found any privacy, she would have thrown a full-fledged temper tantrum, but she couldn't very well do that in front of eight very curious little girls.

Instead, she jerked open a suitcase and snatched out her bathing suit. She was headed back out the door when Jenny stopped her.

"What's the matter? Couldn't you find Dave?" she asked softly.

"I found him, all right," Brittany said angrily. "But it turns out that I didn't have to worry about explaining about last night. It was all just a big joke."

"It couldn't have been. What if I talked to him for you?"

"Don't you dare! So far, you and I are the only ones who know how close I came to making an idiot of myself, and I want to keep it that way." She gestured to the bathing suit she was still clutching in her hand. "I'm going for a swim to cool off."

Because the campers were resting inside their cabins and most of the counselors were at the lake, boating or just lazing around on the pier, Brittany and one of the senior counselors had the pool all to themselves.

She stayed there, swimming laps, until it was time to change back into her clothes and assemble at the recreational field. By then she was so tired that she couldn't even work up any frustration over losing the game.

Afterward, Jenny and Brittany let their girls go to the swimming pool or lake while they went back to their cabin. The scavenger hunt would officially end when the dinner whistle blew, but since they had to serve in the cafeteria, they had to get their things in early.

Brittany checked off each item as she handed it to Jenny, who placed it inside an old pillowcase.

When they'd finished with everything else, Jenny said, "Okay, get the treasure chest, and we'll put it on top."

Brittany pulled out another suitcase and opened it, but the treasure chest wasn't on top where she'd left it. She checked along the sides. Still nothing. She began taking things out of the suitcase and piling them on the floor.

"It's not here," she finally said.

Jenny dropped the pillowcase she was holding. "What do you mean—it's not there?"

"Just what I said. The treasure chest is not in this suitcase."

Jenny started pulling out the other suitcases and emptying them on the floor. "It has to be here somewhere!"

After everything that Brittany owned was spread out on the floor, it was obvious the treasure chest was missing.

"What do you think happened to it?" Brittany asked.

"Somebody must have taken it," Jenny said.

"You mean someone was in our cabin going through my...our things?" Brittany shuttered. "That's scary."

"And against the rules. I wonder if anything else is missing?"

"All the items for the scavenger hunt were here, and none of the girls have mentioned losing any of their personal things. Have you lost anything?"

Jenny shook her head. "No, how about you?"

Brittany looked around her. "I can't think of anything."

Together they started putting her things back. "I think someone is trying to sabotage us," Jenny said. "They trashed the bathroom, stole your clothes, and now this. Maybe it's time we reported what's been going on to the Walkers."

"I don't know. I don't particularly want to tell everyone I lost my clothes, and...I guess I feel funny about claiming someone is picking on us. It would make us look like a bunch of crybabies."

"You're right. Since we kept the treasure chest a big secret from everyone, we can't even prove we ever had it," Jenny said. "But without it, we can't possibly win."

"What about all these other things?" Brittany asked.

"They won't stand up against the treasure chest. It was worth twenty-five points all by itself. I'm just glad that we didn't tell the girls about it. At least they won't be too disappointed about losing.''

''I'd really like to know who took it,'' Brittany said.

''We will,'' Jenny said.

''How?''

''We may not be able to prove it, but the only way anyone can beat us in the scavenger hunt is if they have the treasure chest.''

She handed the pillowcase with the rest of their booty over to Brittany. ''You go ahead and turn these in, and I'll round up the girls and you at the cafeteria.''

On her way from the office, Brittany detoured past the scoreboard to check out the numbers and caught Bill Howland, whose cabin was working with hers in the cafeteria, doing the same thing.

''I don't even know why we even bothered to turn in our things,'' he said. ''We didn't get serious about looking until yesterday, and we couldn't find more than ten things.''

''We looked all week,'' she said. ''With all our demerits, it was our only chance to improve our standing.''

They were still in last place but they weren't too far behind the third- and fourth-place cabins. Glenda's cabin, G1, was in first place, and G3, with Beverly Adams and Carol Smith, was in second. They were so far ahead that Brittany knew Jenny was right. They couldn't possibly win the Best Cabin contest without the treasure chest.

On the boys' side, Dave and Troy were still in first place, but all the boys' scores were within five or ten points of one another. A low score on the scavenger hunt could hurt any of them.

"When will we know who won?" she asked Bill.

"Coach will announce it at the campfire tonight so that the runners-up can choose what they want to do for the banquet."

"Which job would you rather have?"

"It doesn't really matter. My cabin's bound to come in last place and have to take whatever no one else wants," Bill said.

By the time Bill and Brittany reached the cafeteria, their campers were already busy setting the tables. The main course was lasagna, and while Bill and his cabin mate, Tom Leitenberger, handled the large, hot trays of food, Brittany and Jenny served the salad and dessert.

After everyone else had finished eating, they had to return the serving dishes to the kitchen, sweep the floor and wipe off all the tables before they could join the rest of the camp around the campfire.

When they finally took their seats, Coach was getting up to make the big announcement.

"I know you're all anxious to find out who won the scavenger hunt and the contest for the Best Cabins, so other than congratulating all of you on one of the best contests that we've had in recent years, I won't keep you in suspense any longer than necessary."

He moved over to the scoreboard and held up a sheet of paper. "The totals on this board reflect everything you have earned up to this point. I'll add the scores for the scavenger hunt, and we'll see who our winners are."

He started with the lowest score, and Brittany noticed that he went directly to Bill's cabin. From there, he moved around the scoreboard, until he came to the final, highest score.

Before he finished writing their score, the girls from G4 realized they had won the scavenger hunt and started cheering. Jenny and Brittany were too surprised to do anything but stare at each other.

"What happened to the treasure chest?" Brittany whispered to Jenny.

Jenny was still studying the board, and she shook her head. "I don't know. It wasn't even turned in. Look, we came in third place overall, but no one is that far ahead of us."

"It's our custom to honor the top boys' and girls' cabin at a banquet on the last night of camp," Coach was saying. "So tomorrow night, Cabins G1, led by Verna and Glenda, and B1, with Dave and Troy, will be our honored guests."

He waited for the cheers to subside before continuing. "The rest of the cabins will either decorate, serve, clean up or provide the entertainment. When you go by the office to pick up the items you turned in for the scavenger hunt, you can tell Betty which job you prefer. Of course, the second-place cabins get the first choice, and it works backward from there."

"What should we do?" Brittany asked.

"Decorating and serving are the two easiest jobs. Beverly and Carol's cabin came in second, so they get first choice. We can take the one they don't, provided our girls don't want to do the entertainment. It's not exactly work, but..."

"Oh, heavens, let's not even give them that option," Brittany said. "Since I have to go in with the girls, anyway, I'll go by and pick up our things."

"Thanks. I want to go find Troy and congratulate him," Jenny said.

Brittany gathered up their campers and sent them on ahead to get ready for bed while she went to the office. Betty was already there, ready to write down their decision.

"Our first choice is decorating, but if Beverly's cabin chooses that, then we'll serve," Brittany said.

"That's usually the way it goes," Betty replied. "Your cabin did really well. I don't think anyone's ever scored that many points on the scavenger hunt before."

"Thanks. We really worked hard," she said. "But I was wondering... did anyone turn in the treasure chest?"

"No, I guess Charles hid it too well. We'll have to send Dave out to get it so we won't wind up with two treasure chests next week."

That's it, Brittany gasped. *Dave* knew that she'd found the treasure chest. He'd been with her! Maybe he'd have some ideas about what could have happened to it.

She turned to leave, and almost as if her thoughts had conjured him up, she saw Dave standing in the doorway watching her.

"Congratulations," he said. "I knew you were going to win, but I thought you would have made more points with the—"

"Dave!" Glenda called out as she came running up the steps. "Isn't it wonderful?"

"Yeah. It looks like we're going to a banquet together," he said.

Glenda laughed. "If that's an invitation, I accept."

Brittany knew she wouldn't get a chance to talk to Dave with Glenda around, so slipped silently away. She would wait along the path and catch him on his way back to his cabin.

Dave saw her leave and started to follow, but Glenda put her hand out to stop him. He started to brush it away, but the flash of her ring caught his eye, and he stopped. Why did the ring look so familiar to him?

"Didn't you forget to get your things?" Glenda asked.

"I guess I did," he admitted sheepishly.

Once they were inside the office, he took advantage of the brighter light to get a better look at the ring. He had seen it before, and now he knew where. On Brittany's hand.

Brittany wouldn't have given away a ring that her uncle had made for her, and there was certainly no reason for her to sell it. So how did Glenda get it?

His aunt handed them their things, and Dave swung his over his shoulder. "Come on," he said to Glenda. "I'll walk you back as far as I'm allowed to go."

"Well, thank you." She smiled. "I'm surprised you aren't hurrying to catch up with Brittany."

"Why would you think that?"

"Don't try to play innocent with me, Dave Walker! You're just as guilty of chasing after that girl as every other boy in camp."

So much for the idea that she had borrowed the ring from Brittany, he thought. They obviously weren't that friendly. He couldn't just come out and ask her about it—not until he was sure that she trusted him.

"Is that what you thought?" he asked, taking her hand.

"It's what I know," Glenda said less vehemently.

"If you really wanted to know what I was up to, you should have asked."

"All right. I'm asking you now."

"Brittany and Troy had a bet that she wouldn't stick it out for a whole week," Dave said, improvising quickly. "Troy had me keeping an eye on her. He wanted to know how close she was to breaking."

"And that's all?"

"What else would it be? You couldn't think I was interested in that . . . that spoiled brat."

"Well, it did occur to me," Glenda said, laughing softly up at him.

They were so involved with each other that neither of them noticed the silent figure standing in the shadows.

Chapter Ten

Spoiled brat!

Brittany could feel her heart pounding in her chest, but she forced herself to stand completely still until Dave and Glenda were far enough ahead that they wouldn't see her step back onto the path.

She hadn't meant to eavesdrop. She was just waiting for a chance to ask Dave about the treasure chest. When she saw him with Glenda, she'd stepped back into the shadows, and now she was glad that she had.

Spoiled brat, indeed! Hadn't she stuck it out the whole week? She'd gotten up early, worked in the infirmary, helped clean the bathroom and served meals—all without complaining, or at least not very loudly.

Her cabin had worked hard to win the scavenger hunt, and if the treasure chest hadn't disappeared, they would have won the Best Cabin contest, too!

She stormed back to her cabin, too upset to even notice if she passed anyone along the way. It was all she could do to stay reasonably calm long enough to make sure the girls were all accounted for and tucked into bed before the last whistle sounded.

Once the lights were out, she stretched out in bed, and little by little released the tight control she had kept on her emotions. She'd expected a flood of tears to follow, but instead, she remained dry-eyed.

Spoiled. Dave had called her spoiled. Of course, it wasn't the first time she had heard that particular word used to describe her. Troy had always called her that, but she'd never taken him seriously. Dave was different. This week, he'd acted as if he really cared how she felt and what she thought. He wouldn't have called her a spoiled brat unless he really meant it.

What was worse—she knew he was right. Her whole family spoiled her, and she let them. Maybe she didn't whine or throw temper tantrums, but it was only because she never had to resort to such tactics to get her way. She let her family, her grandparents, aunts, uncles and even cousins cater to her and wait on her until the only thing they expected from her was for her to smile and look pretty.

Was it possible for her to change? Tomorrow was her last full day at camp, and for Jenny's and her campers' sakes, she was going to make it a good one. No more feeling like a martyr simply because she had to follow the same rules and regulations set for everyone else. She was a counselor, here to set an example and show the younger children how to get the most out of camp.

When her alarm went off the next morning, Brittany rolled out of bed and started dressing before she even remembered the resolution she had made the night before. Maybe it wasn't going to be so hard to change, after all. She'd already made some progress.

At breakfast, Coach announced that the cabins that were providing the entertainment at the banquet could stay to plan and rehearse their performance, but the rest of them would hike to the other side of the lake.

It was on the tip of Brittany's tongue to ask how far it was and if everyone had to go, but she kept quiet. While everyone else helped out by carrying some of the picnic supplies, Betty gave her a knapsack of extra medical supplies to carry with them.

They started out from the flagpole, and even though each cabin stayed together, it was a loosely organized group. Jenny and Troy positioned themselves so that they could walk together, but Brittany stayed at the rear of their group, as far away as possible from her cousin and his cabin mate. Besides, she was comfortable walking with Bill Howland.

"I don't know whether a seven-mile hike is a reward or punishment," he commented.

"Seven miles! Are you sure?" she asked.

"That's what someone told me last year, and I don't think the lake has gotten any smaller."

"We may be exhausted when we get back, but I'd rather go on this hike than have to entertain at the banquet tonight," she said.

"I agree," Bill said. "I was so sure that my cabin was going to have to do that, but luckily for us, Sean's cabin decided they wanted to entertain."

Most of the time they walked in companionable silence, saving their energy for the path. On the whole, most of the younger campers seemed to be having more fun than some of the counselors, but Brittany noticed that no one complained when Coach finally called a rest period.

She had just slipped off her pack and was sinking to the ground beside Bill when Dave walked up.

She refused to meet his eye until he asked, "Have you got any Band-Aids in that first-aid pack of yours?"

"Of course." She was already reaching for her pack. "What's the problem?"

"I've got a kid with a blister."

She started to get up, but he shook his head. "Just give me the Band-Aid, and I'll put it on him myself."

"I'd better do it," she said. "I have to look at it so that I can make a note of it in my journal."

He offered her his hand, but Brittany ignored it and pushed herself off the ground.

As they made their way back to his little group, Dave lowered his voice so that only she could hear. "Is something wrong?"

Brittany kept her face averted, refusing to meet his eyes. "What makes you ask that?"

"I don't know. You're different."

"I would have thought you'd find that an improvement," she snapped.

Dave took her arm, forcing her to turn around and face him. "What's that supposed to mean?"

"Forget it. It doesn't matter, anyway."

"Yes, it does. I want—"

"Over here," Troy called impatiently.

Brittany pulled away from Dave and went over to kneel down beside Troy, surprised to see the little boy she had brought to camp with her.

"Bobby, I haven't seen you all week. How've you been?"

"Okay until now," he said. "You aren't going to hurt me, are you?"

"Of course not," she assured him. "Just let me have a look at that blister."

He held up his foot, and Brittany could see that the skin was red and irritated. A small blister the size of a pencil eraser had formed on his heel.

Explaining her procedure step-by-step, she cleaned the area and bandaged it. "When we get back to camp, I want you to go to the infirmary and let whoever's on duty check it out again," she said.

Bobby nodded, pulling his sock and shoe back on as Brittany stood up to leave. "As long as the Band-Aid stays in place, walking shouldn't bother him, but let me know if he has any more trouble," she told her cousin.

"I'm impressed," Troy said.

Brittany paused and raised her eyebrows a quarter of an inch. "Because I know how to apply a Band-Aid?"

"No, it's your whole attitude. I'm ready to concede that you came through this week better than I ever thought you would."

"Really?"

Troy looped his arm around her shoulder. "When have you ever known me to say anything nice that I didn't mean, especially to you?"

"You've got a point." She laughed, leaning into him.

He gave her a brief hug and said, "You're all right, cuz."

Troy's rare compliment gave her such a lift that it helped to carry her through the second leg of the hike until it was time to stop for lunch.

When Coach finally signaled them to stop, it was a toss-up whether they were more hungry or tired. The younger campers recuperated first and began setting out the picnic supplies. By the time everyone was ready, Brittany realized she was ravenous.

She took a couple of sandwiches and a drink and found a shady spot under a tree beside Bill and George Howland.

"Is it all right if I join you?" Sandy Cross asked, just as Brittany was getting settled. "I don't exactly fit in with the college group, and I think I might be intruding if I tried to join either of them," she said, gesturing to where Jenny and Troy and Dave and Glenda were sitting slightly apart from everyone else.

Bill laid his head on Brittany's shoulder. "How do you know you're not intruding here?" he asked.

Brittany quickly shrugged his head away and made room for Sandy. "Don't pay him any attention," she said.

"You can sit here with me," George invited.

Sandy sat down and stretched out her legs. "Thanks. I don't think I could have stood much longer," she said. "Will you look at the way those kids are running around? A few minutes ago, my girls were begging me to let them stop. They said they couldn't walk another step."

"I heard the same thing," George said.

For the next few minutes, no one tried to talk as they concentrated on their lunch. And then, after they were satisfied, they stretched out on the grass and watched the children as they ran around chasing one another or waded in the shallow water along the edge of the lake.

All too soon, Coach announced that it was time to gather up all their trash and finish the hike back to camp. In spite of the angry protests from her muscles, Brittany got up and started moving around.

Surprisingly enough, once they got started, she found that it really wasn't that bad. The return didn't seem as long or tiring, and they got back to camp in plenty of time for everyone to go swimming.

Ordinarily, Brittany would have left the water in time to wash and dry her hair before dinner, but today it just didn't seem that important. When it was time to go to the cafeteria, she rinsed it under the hose and then combed it out, leaving it damp against her shoulders. After all, it wasn't as though no one had ever seen her with wet hair before.

"Do we have to serve everybody's dinner tonight?" Pam asked as they walked to the cafeteria to get ready for the banquet.

"No. We only have to serve the head table. Everyone else will go through the buffet line as always."

"I don't mind helping with the buffet line, but I don't want to wait on tables," Jada said.

"I do," Melba said. "I'm going to spill a whole plate of food in someone's lap—accidentally of course."

"Don't you dare," Jenny said.

"Why not?" Judy asked.

"If we go in there with long faces and looking miserable, it's just going to make them feel that much more superior. If you really want to get back at them, pretend you're having more fun than they are," Jenny said.

"That's right," Marlene said. "They'll start wishing they had come in third."

Brittany stopped at the door and faced the rest of the group, holding up her hands. "Once you pass through this door, nothing but smiles. Agreed?"

"Agreed!" they shouted back.

She pushed open the door, and for a minute they all stopped and stared. The cafeteria had been completely transformed.

The tables had been rearranged so that they all faced the head tables, which were lavishly decorated with wildflowers, candles and even tablecloths. It really did look like a banquet.

In spite of her good intentions, Brittany muttered, "Darn!"

"What's the matter?" Jenny asked.

"I just realized how much I want to be at the head table," she said.

"I know that, and you know that, but we can't let anyone else know. After the way Glenda Camp was gloating today, I want her to wish she was serving instead."

"You don't really believe we can do that, do you?" Brittany asked.

"No, but it'll make her wonder what we're up to."

Brittany laughed and realized that Jenny was right. Just pretending to have a good time lightened her spirits. The only real difficulty she had was when Dave walked in and took a seat beside Glenda.

"I think your cousin is enjoying this," Jenny whispered to Brittany as she picked up the pitcher of water to refill Troy's glass for the third time.

"So is Glenda," Brittany returned.

Glenda had asked for more ice, a fresh napkin and another clean set of silverware, but each time, Brittany had managed to send over one of the younger girls. Her only contact with them had been when she served their plates, and though she refused to acknowledge it, she had heard Dave murmur his thanks.

But the strain of keeping up a happy face was both physically and emotionally draining. Even though the two last-place cabins put on a good show with funny skits and fast-moving songs, Brittany was glad when it was over.

As soon as the applause died down, she told Jenny, "I know this is supposed to be my night off, but why don't you go ahead and take it."

"Thanks, but Troy has to go in, anyway. Wouldn't you like to stay out for a little while at least? This is your last night."

Brittany shook her head. "I've got a lot of packing to do. Besides, I think I've seen Glenda and Dave together enough for one day," she said.

"I'm not so sure they're really together. I watched Dave at the picnic today. He couldn't keep his eyes off your little group."

"Well, I'm sure he wasn't watching me."

"How do you know?"

"I just do." Brittany couldn't bring herself to tell Jenny about the conversation she had overheard between Glenda and Dave.

Dave was instantly aware when Brittany and Jenny left, and in a strange way, he was relieved. It was hard for him to concentrate on anyone else when Brittany was around, and since she was leaving tomorrow, he had to find out something about her ring.

Glenda hadn't worn it on the hike today, but she had it on now, and he couldn't let her get away until he asked about it. Purposely, he took her hand and led her over to sit on a log beside the fire.

He waited until some of the other counselors had drifted away, and then, still holding her hand, he studied the ring in the firelight.

Finally, he asked, "What kind of ring is this?"

"Oh, it's nothing." She laughed lightly and tried to pull her hand away, but Dave held on to it firmly.

"What do you mean? I think it's pretty."

"Believe it or not, I found it. I was going to throw it away, but I decided to keep it and wear it for fun."

"Found? You mean here at camp?"

"Actually it was inside the treasure chest."

Dave dropped her hand. "*You* found the treasure chest? But Brittany..."

"Don't tell me she told you that she'd found it," Glenda said.

"Uh, no, she didn't tell me anything. Her cabin won the scavenger hunt, so I just assumed that they had the chest."

"I didn't turn it in," Glenda explained. "My cabin was already so far ahead we didn't need it."

"What did you do with it?"

"I put it away. This ring is really the only thing worth keeping."

Dave bent down and picked up a twig and tossed it onto the glowing embers of the fire. He was afraid to look at Glenda, afraid that she might be able to see what he was thinking. The treasure chest was the key to this whole puzzle, but he didn't have much time left to figure it all out. He had to get some help.

Out of the corner of his eye, Dave saw his uncle coming to check on the campfire, and he stood up quickly. "Uncle Charles, did Aunt Betty tell you about those boxes?" he asked.

His uncle frowned. "What boxes?" he asked.

Dave tried to look sufficiently upset. "The ones I was supposed to take to her office before dinner," he said. "Glenda, I'm sorry, but I have to go take care of that now. Aunt Betty said she needed to pack up some of her things tonight, and if I don't get her those boxes, she might pack me up, too."

"Do you want me to go on to my cabin, or should I wait here?" Glenda asked.

"No, wait for me here," he said, afraid that she might take off the ring if she went back to her cabin. "I'll be back as soon as I've seen Aunt Betty."

Chapter Eleven

While Dave was in his aunt's office, explaining the various pieces of the puzzle and trying to figure out how they fitted together, Brittany was trying to figure out how to get all her things back into her suitcases.

"You know it would help if we could turn on some lights," she complained to Jenny who was holding a flashlight for her.

"And get caught being up after lights-out," Jenny said. "No thank you."

"But if I don't get this done tonight, I'll never be ready to leave on time tomorrow."

"I wish you weren't leaving."

"I'm glad you feel that way. I was afraid you were going to want to throw me out after the first day."

"After the first day, I did." Jenny laughed. "But I'm glad we learned how to work things out."

A light knock at the door interrupted them, and Jenny immediately switched off her flashlight.

"Get in bed," she whispered to Brittany and started sneaking back across the room to her own bed. Brittany was still fully dressed, but when the knock came again, she slid under the covers.

Across the room, Jenny called out, "Yes, who is it?"

By this time, several of the campers were sitting up in their beds, and they all had to shade their eyes as Mrs. Clark flipped on the overhead light and stepped inside the room.

"Betty wants to see the counselors in her office. I'm here to stay with your girls until you get back," she said.

"Is something wrong?" Brittany asked, getting up.

The sight of Brittany rising, fully dressed, from her bed, disconcerted Mrs. Clark enough that it took her a moment to collect her thoughts. "No...not really...she just wants to talk to you."

"Let me get into some clothes," Jenny said, already beginning to pull things from her duffel bag while Brittany reached for a brush to do her hair.

"What's this all about?" Brittany asked as she and Jenny made their way to the office. "Do they usually have a debriefing at the end of camp?"

"This is the first one I've known anything about."

"We haven't done anything wrong, have we?"

"Not that I know of," Jenny answered.

As they made their way up the steps to the office, they could see Glenda and her cabin mate already there, looking as confused as they felt.

"Come on in, girls," Betty said. "I'm sorry to bring you out tonight, but since tomorrow is the last day of the first week of camp and Brittany will be leaving us, I had to get you together so that I could ask Brittany if she has a ring like the one Glenda's wearing."

Glenda gasped, and as they all turned to look at her left hand, she instinctively covered it with the right.

"Could we see your ring, Glenda?" Betty asked.

Slowly, Glenda extended her hand, and Brittany recognized the golden nugget. She looked from Glenda to Betty and then back again. "That's my ring," she said. "I mean, I think it is. I have one just like that."

"Do you know where it is right now?"

"I thought it was back in my cabin. I took it off right after I got here, and I haven't worn it since."

"Do you know anything about the ring, Jenny?" Betty asked.

"Not really. I know Brittany brought some jewelry with her. I've seen her jewelry box, but I can't honestly say I recognize the ring."

"I don't remember putting it in my jewelry box," Brittany said. "I think I just slipped it inside one of my suitcases."

"Is there any way either of you can prove whether or not the ring is yours?" Betty asked.

"Mine has my initials on the inside," Brittany said.

Betty held out her hand to Glenda. "May I see the ring?"

Glenda pulled the ring off her finger and handed it to Betty without looking at it.

"B.A.A.," Betty read slowly.

"That's mine," Brittany said. "Brittany Ann Allen."

"I didn't steal it!" Glenda insisted.

"Then how did you get it?" Betty asked.

"I...I took it, but I didn't know—I mean, I thought it was part of the costume jewelry from the treasure chest. I was just playing a trick on them. I didn't mean to take anything valuable."

Betty looked at Verna Kane, Glenda's cabin mate, and asked, "Did you know anything about this?"

Verna shook her head. "I knew that she trashed the bathroom and hid Brittany's clothes one morning, and I told her to cool it, but I didn't know anything about this."

"I wasn't trying to steal anything. I was just going to take some of the items they found for the scavenger hunt."

"Going into someone's cabin and taking *anything* is a serious infraction. In fact, you've actually committed a crime," Betty said.

"But it wasn't fair for them to win the Best Cabin contest," Glenda said. "Our cabin had the most points in everything else. Why should they win just because they found a stupid chest?"

"No," Betty said, "you can't justify your actions by claiming that we were wrong. I believe that the rules for our contest are fair, but if you had a problem with them, you should have come to us, not taken matters into your own hands."

"Yes, Mrs. Walker. I'm very sorry," Glenda said.

"I'm sorry, too," Betty sighed.

She handed the ring back to Brittany and said, "I wish I could do more than just return your ring, but unfortunately it's too late to give your campers the banquet they deserve. I will announce what happened at breakfast tomorrow morning. At least everyone will know that you won the contest."

Brittany slipped the ring on her finger. "I'm glad to have my ring back, especially since I didn't even know it was missing, but I'd rather you didn't make any announcement. I think it would be better to leave things the way they are. I don't want our girls going away forgetting how much fun we had and only remembering that they were cheated out of a banquet."

"I agree," Jenny said. "Our girls didn't even know we'd found the treasure chest. We were going to surprise them with it when we won."

"I think that's very understanding of you," Betty said. "You can go back to your cabin now. You, too, Verna. I want to talk to Glenda alone."

Outside the office, Verna turned to them. "I'm sorry about what happened, kids. If I'd known about it, I would have put a stop to it."

"It's okay," Jenny said.

She and Brittany turned toward their own cabin, and Brittany said, "The only person that I'd really like to tell is Troy. I want him to know that our cabin really won the Best Cabin contest.''

"He probably already knows. Dave is his cabin mate, and since he was with you when you found the treasure chest, I'm sure he told Troy."

"He told Glenda, you mean," Brittany said.

"You don't really believe that."

"How do you think she knew we had the treasure chest? We didn't tell anyone."

"I don't know, but—"

"Come on," Brittany interrupted. "I don't want to think about it anymore. Besides, I still have to finish packing."

Brittany awoke the next morning feeling sluggish and out of sorts. Even the girls were more subdued than usual as they rolled up their sleeping bags and stacked them beside the door with their suitcases. It was their last morning together, their last breakfast, but no one wanted to talk about that. Instead they talked about their families and plans for the rest of the summer.

They were just leaving their cabin for the morning ceremony when Betty stopped them. "The rest of you go on. I want to talk to Brittany," she said.

"Is something wrong?" Brittany asked.

"No, it's nothing like that, I promise. I just wanted to check with you to see if you were still planning to let Bobby Wayne ride back home in your car."

"Sure, he's no problem. Is that all?"

"Not exactly. You see, Glenda won't be staying on as a counselor, and even with Barbara Holland coming in to replace you, that's still going to leave us one counselor short. I know our agreement was just for you to work one week, but Charles and I wondered if you would consider staying longer."

"You mean, you want me to stay?"

"Of course. You've done a great job, and we'd be happy to keep you all summer if you'd want the job. You could even stay in the same cabin with Jenny if you want to."

"Do I? It would be wonderful. I'd accept right now, but I really should talk to my father."

"We'll only be in town long enough for everyone to have lunch and for us to pick up the next load of campers. Why don't you go ahead and call him from the office? That will give him more time to think about it."

"Thanks, and I'll still drive Bobby home. If Dad says I can come back, I'll just ride back on the bus, like everyone else," she called back as she hurried to the office.

Her father answered on the second ring, and although he wanted the extra time to think about it, he seemed pleased that she liked the camp and wanted to stay longer.

She was confident enough in her ability to convince him to let her stay that she couldn't wait to find Jenny and share the news with her. The morning ceremony was just ending, and Brittany caught up with her on the way to the cafeteria.

"Guess what? I'm staying!"

Jenny stopped and stared at her. "You're what?"

As they made their way through the cafeteria line, Brittany gave her the details and finished with "Betty said I could stay in the same cabin. Is that all right with you?"

"It's great! I won't have to break in another cabin mate."

"Dad said he would have to think about it and let me know when I got home, but I'm sure he'll let me stay. In fact, why don't you come have lunch with me and help me convince him?"

"Thanks, but when I told Troy that my parents were going to be at my grandmother's in Flagstaff this weekend, he invited me to have lunch with him and his family."

"That's the same thing," Brittany said. "I'm sure our families will be together."

When they finished breakfast, the campers rushed out to take some last-minute pictures and exchange addresses with some of their other friends, and Brittany began repacking her suitcases.

"Why are you doing that if you're coming back?" Jenny asked.

"I just thought I'd take back a few of the nonessentials."

Jenny clutched her heart. "What!" she exclaimed, "Brittany Allen is going to wear the same pair of shoes two days in a row?"

"Oh, stop that, and help me get this stuff sorted," Brittany told her, pretending to be cross.

Jenny helped her get them into a suitcase and said, "Well, if we keep weeding through this stuff every week, by the end of the summer, you should have a manageable amount."

"Very funny." Brittany struggled to get the suitcase out of the door.

"Do you need some help?" a familiar voice asked.

Brittany looked up and saw Dave standing in front of her.

"No, thank you," she said.

She attempted to walk past him, but he fell into step with her. And after watching her struggle for a few yards, he tried again. "That suitcase looks really heavy. Are you sure—"

"I can manage just fine."

Eventually, she had to set the suitcase down to rest, and when she did, Dave snatched it up and stalked away. There wasn't anything she could do without making a scene, so she followed sullenly.

He set the suitcase down beside her car and waited for her to unlock the trunk. "Is this the last one?" he asked.

She didn't want him to know it was the *only* one, so she answered spitefully, "Yes, I've already loaded everything else. Why don't you put that on the floorboard behind the driver's seat? Bobby can spread his sleeping bag on the back seat if he wants to sleep."

Bill Howland, on his way to the buses, stopped by the car and said, "Hey, Brittany, I'll be your escort."

"Thanks, I..."

"She already has one," Dave said.

Brittany flashed him an angry look, but she waited until Bill left before saying bluntly, "I don't want you to ride with me."

"I'm so sorry, but you can't always have things the way you want them," he said.

"Why not?"

"It just doesn't work that way. Look, Brittany, I know you've been avoiding me, but we have to talk sometime, and it might as well be now. Besides, as a representative of Camp Chabewa, I have to ride with Bobby to guarantee his safety."

She started to say something and then changed her mind and walked off.

Since there was no rule about having a Chabewa representative riding with her, Dave watched to see where she was going. He knew that his aunt or uncle would let her choose whoever she wanted to ride with her.

Fortunately she didn't go toward the office. He leaned against the side of the car to wait for her, and lost in thought, he didn't realize what had happened until Troy walked up, the car keys dangling from his hand.

Dave looked around for Brittany and spotted her disappearing up the steps of the bus.

Chapter Twelve

The camp bus was as noisy and bumpy as Brittany had expected, but the trip itself wasn't nearly as bad as she had feared. She spent most of the time exchanging addresses with the girls from her cabin and promising to write each of them.

When they reached the outskirts of town and had to slow down for the traffic that clogged the main freeways, she was surprised to discover how different things seemed after only a week at camp. Everything seemed so irritatingly close, and the air, coming through the open windows, was heavy with the odor of automobile exhaust fumes.

As soon as they pulled into the Oak Grove High School parking lot and she saw her father waiting for her, Brittany forgot all about her displeasure with the trappings of civilization. She was overwhelmed with a rush of happiness. Now she was just as anxious to get off the bus as any of the children.

At first, she couldn't find her father anywhere in the crowd. She was beginning to believe that she had only imagined seeing him, and then she realized where he must be. He must have gone to her car.

She made her way past the buses and, as she had suspected, saw him standing beside her car talking to Troy and Dave.

"Dad," she called, running over to be engulfed in his open arms.

"Well, at least you didn't completely forget me."

"Of course I didn't. Why would you say that?"

"You did call to ask if you could stay at camp for the rest of the summer," he reminded her.

"May I? Have you made up your mind yet?"

"I don't have any objections, but I had a hard time convincing the rest of the family. They finally decided that if you looked happy enough, they wouldn't argue. They're all waiting for you at Granny's."

"Aunt Helen, too?"

"Yes, she said for me to bring Troy with us."

"Good. He can drive my car, and I'll ride with you," Brittany said and then remembered to ask. "That is . . . if that's all right with you?"

"It's fine," Troy said. "I'll go drag Jenny out of that crowd and be right behind you."

"Who's Jenny?" Frank Allen asked.

"My cabin mate," Brittany explained. "She's wonderful. You'll love her—Troy does."

"Brittany!" Troy said.

"I can see some things have changed," Mr. Allen said. Dave had been standing quietly off to one side, and Frank included him. "How about joining us for lunch?"

Brittany allowed herself one quick glance in his direction. When she found him looking back at her, she quickly averted her eyes again.

"Thanks, but my parents are expecting me," Dave said.

"I understand. If I don't hurry up and get home, Brittany's grandmothers and aunts are liable to come over here looking for us," Frank Allen said, nudging Brittany toward his car.

On the way to her grandmother's, Brittany kept up a running monologue about camp. She knew the episode with Glenda would worry him needlessly, so she wisely left that out. Besides, it had already been settled, and there were plenty of other good things to talk about.

When they pulled into her grandmother's driveway, Brittany hopped out of the car and was immediately surrounded by her whole family. With hugs and kisses, they led her through the house and to the dining room, where the table was already set with all her favorite foods.

With the fuss that everyone was making, she didn't even know when Troy and Jenny had arrived, but she saw them with Aunt Helen, across the table from her, and smiled.

For dessert, Granny brought out a tray with six different kinds of sweets. "I couldn't decide what to make for you, so I just made a variety," she said.

"Granny, I can't eat another thing." Brittany sighed.

"Then I'll put them in a tin so that you can take them with you. They'll be good later on."

"Will they ever," she said. "They probably won't last the night."

"I'm glad I'm your cabin mate," Jenny said.

"Granny, don't forget to make a care package for me, too," Troy said.

"I won't," she said, disappearing into the kitchen.

"When Frank said you were going back to camp, I brought over a couple of new outfits I thought you might like," Cecelia said. "If you don't like them, I'll take them back."

"Aunt Cecelia, you didn't have to do that."

"What about money?" Ernestine asked. "Do you have enough?"

"I'm fine," she insisted. "Remember, I'm getting paid for working."

"And your car?" Ed asked.

"I won't be taking it back with me this time. I'll ride the bus."

"Then I'll take it to the shop and give it a good going-over before you get back," he said.

The farewells took almost as long as the entire visit, but eventually, Frank had to drive them back to the school parking lot.

"I can't believe the fuss they made just because you've been gone for a week," Jenny said after they got out of the car.

"Are you kidding?" Troy said. "It's like that every time they see her. Even if it's only been a day."

Jenny shook her head. "It's a wonder you're as down-to-earth as you are. That kind of treatment could really warp you."

"I thought it already had," Troy said, "but I don't know. She may not be completely spoiled, after all. After last week, I'm beginning to think there may still be some hope for her."

Brittany smiled back at him. "You just wait. I'll show you yet."

"We'd better check in and get our bus assignments," Jenny said.

"I'll do it for all of us," Troy said. "You two can mill around and see if anyone needs help."

There were plenty of people in need of help, and until the last minute, all the counselors stayed busy helping the new campers load their bags, finding the right bus and answering their parents' questions about the food, sleeping arrangements and participation requirements.

As soon as the last camper climbed on the bus, Jenny called, "Come on, Brittany. We're riding this bus."

Brittany ran up the steps, but when she started to follow Jenny to the back, Troy blocked her path.

"All the counselors can't sit together, and if you don't mind, I'd like to sit with Jenny."

"Okay." She grinned. "I'll sit up front, but you owe me one."

She turned around and started back up the aisle and saw Dave climbing up the steps. He picked up his chart from the front seat and said, "You can sit here."

Brittany saw an empty space directly behind him. "No thank you. I'll sit here," she said.

After he'd turned away, she leaned over to the little girl in the seat beside her and asked, "Is it all right if I sit with you?"

The little girl gave a jerky nod, and Brittany thought she detected a choked sob. "My name's Brittany," she said. "What's yours?"

"Samantha Dueit, but everyone calls me Sam."

"Is anything wrong? Maybe I can help."

"I...I've never been...to camp before. I'm scared."

Brittany nodded. "I know what you mean. Last week was my first week at camp, and I was scared, too."

"You were?"

"Yes, but do you know what? I liked it so much, I decided to come back."

"What's it like?"

"Well... have you ever been to a slumber party?"

Sam nodded, and Brittany smiled. "Well, it's kind of like a slumber party that lasts for a whole week."

Sam brightened a little and said shyly, "Will you be with me all the time?"

"I don't know. You see, everyone is assigned to a cabin, and..." She paused and took a deep breath. Dave had the information she needed, and although she was still reluctant to talk to him, it would ease Sam's mind to know.

She leaned forward and tapped him on the shoulder. "Excuse me, but could you tell me if Samantha Dueit is in my cabin?"

"Are you and Jenny going to be in the same cabin?" he asked, running his finger down the list of names.

"Yes, cabin four," she answered.

Dave stopped at Samantha's name and shook his head. "She's assigned to G2."

Sam groaned, and Brittany reached over and patted her sympathetically. "Is there any way to switch her to my cabin?" she asked Dave.

Dave's eyebrows went up, and he started to shake his head but changed his mind. "I'll take care of it for you."

"See, it's going to be all right," Brittany said, smiling brightly at Sam.

"Are you sure? I mean, can he really fix it?" Sam asked.

"You can trust him," Brittany assured her.

Someone from the back of the bus started singing, and the song quickly spread throughout the bus. By the time they turned into the entrance of Camp Chabewa, they had been through all the camp songs that anyone knew—twice.

When the bus came to a stop, Dave handed Brittany his chart and said, "You can give the campers their cabin numbers while I start unloading their luggage. Just keep Samantha with you until I have time to get her switched."

Brittany barely had time to reply before the first kid was off the bus.

"Where do I go?" he asked.

"What's your name?"

"Richard Abbot."

She consulted the list. "You're in B4. That's the next to the last cabin over that way. Look for the numbers over the door."

He nodded and trudged off to get his luggage, and Brittany turned to the next child.

Jenny worked her way through the crowd and finally got Brittany's attention. "I'll go to the cabin and get the girls settled in."

Brittany nodded and pointed to Sam. "Take this one with you."

Sam looked at her questioningly, and Brittany smiled. "It's okay. Tell Jenny to give you the bunk beside my bed, and I'll see you in a few minutes," she said.

When the bus was finally empty, Brittany started toward the office to turn in the chart and met Dave on the path.

"I switched Samantha to your cabin," he said.

"That's good," she replied flippantly. "I've already sent her on to my cabin."

"Is that all you can say?" Dave exploded. "Do you realize what I had to go through to make that one change! The cabin assignments are made weeks in advance, and I had to go through the whole list and find another nine-year-old first-time camper who didn't have a special request or assignment."

"You never mentioned that it was so complicated. How was I supposed to know?"

"I guess you wouldn't. You're so used to people jumping to do whatever you say that you don't even think about what you're putting them through."

Before Brittany could think of a reply, he took the chart from her and stalked away in the direction of the office.

Obviously, she had been right about him all along. He'd just tolerated her for Troy's sake, but now, since he'd probably just discovered that Glenda wasn't coming back and it was somehow her fault, he wasn't pretending any longer.

She turned to go to her own cabin and saw Troy blocking her path. "We have to talk," he said.

"About what?"

"I promised myself that I wouldn't get involved in any of this, but someone has got to tell you what an idiot you're being."

"I don't know what you're talking about!"

"What about the way you're treating Dave?"

"Me treating him? What about the way that he's taken advantage of me? Why don't you ask him how

Glenda knew that Jenny and I had found the treasure chest?''

"Why don't you ask Betty how she knew that Glenda had your ring?'' Troy countered.

Brittany gasped.

Seeing the astonishment on her face, Troy softened his attack. "Dave didn't know Glenda had taken that chest. He was trying to find out what she was doing with your ring, and when she started talking about having the treasure chest, he went straight to his aunt with everything.''

"I guess I owe him an apology, huh?''

"I don't believe you," he said, shaking his head. "You use him, treat him like dirt and then think a simple apology is going to make everything all right. It might not work this time.''

"I know, but I still have to do it. I owe him that much," she said, before adding, "and thanks. Thanks for telling me.''

She should go help Jenny get their girls settled in, but she knew Jenny could handle things there, and it was important that she talk to Dave right away. Of course Troy was probably right. Dave probably didn't want to have anything else to do with her, but he deserved an apology, and he was going to get it.

She saw him coming up the path, and nervously she called out to him, "Dave, could I talk to you?''

He glanced at her and then off toward his cabin. "I have to go check on my boys . . .''

"Troy's already gone over there, and I'll only take a few minutes. Please.''

"Okay, what?"

She swallowed past the lump that had caught in her throat and managed to say, "I just found out that you were the one who got my ring back for me, and I wanted to thank you."

"You're welcome," he said, emotionless.

"I'm sorry I've been so rude to you, but I thought you told Glenda that I found the treasure chest just to make sure that Jenny and I didn't win the Best Cabin contest."

"You really thought I would do something like that?"

"I didn't know what to think. You were the only one who knew that I'd found the chest, and..."

"According to Aunt Betty, Glenda didn't even know you had the treasure chest. She just stumbled on it when she was going through your things to find out how well you were doing. If you don't believe me, talk to Aunt Betty."

"I believe you. I never would have thought otherwise, but I know what you think of me."

Dave looked surprised. "You do?"

"I know I'm a spoiled brat, but I really am trying to change."

"Who asked you to?"

Her voice trembled, and she blinked quickly to hold back the tears. "I thought...I mean, I hoped we could be friends."

"Don't you know?" he asked softly.

"What?"

He stepped off the path and drew Brittany to him behind one of the large trees. "I want to be more than a friend," he said.

Brittany pulled back, but she kept her hands on his shoulders. "I thought you weren't interested in whether or not I tried to change," she said.

"No," Dave said, shaking his head. "I meant that I didn't care whether you changed or not. I like you just the way you are."

"You mean, you don't think that I'm spoiled?"

"Uh-uh." He chuckled. "I know you're spoiled."

Brittany stiffened, but before she could break away, Dave added, "I also know that you're not mean or bad tempered, and that you really care about people."

"I do," she said, relaxing against him. "I care about you."

Dave leaned down and she met him in a kiss.

"I don't know how much more I could have taken," he murmured against her hair. "Having you angry was ten times worse than being ignored by you."

"When did I ever ignore you?"

"Ever since I first started hanging around. You never even gave me a glance."

"That's because you were Troy's friend. He was always telling me what a pest I was, so I thought you felt the same way."

"I guess you have a lot to learn about me."

"No time like the present," said Brittany.

He could feel her lips beneath his curving in a smile.

WATCH FOR THESE TITLES FROM FIRST LOVE COMING NEXT MONTH

A RISKY BUSINESS
Janice Harrell

When Mary Ann and Adam decide to do a little detective work on the neighbors, they end up finding more than they'd bargained for—and not only about the neighbors.

ALLEY CAT
Lee Wardlaw

Why did Alley Cat, KTUNE's sexy new disk jockey with the sultry voice, turn down all public appearances? Was it just part of her act, or was she at heart a little scaredy-cat?

SOMETHING TO TREASURE
Judi Cross

Had prosaic computer-buff David really seen a mermaid, or had he flipped his disk? Already she had him swimming in circles! Was it too late to reprogram?

THE BOY IN WHITE
Tessa Kay

Why did a gorgeous stranger persist in following Kate all around the beautiful island of Corfu? Was he looking for trouble—or romance?